DAISY MILLER
and other stories

DAISY MILLER
and other stories

—————————◆—————————

Henry James

WORDSWORTH CLASSICS

The paper in this book is produced from pure wood pulp, without the use of chlorine or any other substance harmful to the environment. The energy used in its production consists almost entirely of hydroelectricity and heat generated from waste material, thereby conserving fossil fuels and contributing little to the greenhouse effect.

This edition published 1994 by
Wordsworth Editions Limited
Cumberland House, Crib Street
Ware, Hertfordshire SG12 9ET

ISBN 1 85326 213 7

Printed and bound in Denmark by Nørhaven
Typeset in the UK by Antony Gray

INTRODUCTION

Sometimes referred to as a novelette, being halfway between a long short story and a short novel, *Daisy Miller* (1878) represents quintessential Henry James in both its style and its theme and is therefore required reading for all those who seek even a basic understanding and appreciation of Henry James's novels. The book deals with the visit to Europe, in company with her wealthy, conventional and anodyne mother, of the 'strikingly, and admirably pretty' eponymous girl from Schenectady, one of James's finest and most charming portraits of 'the American girl', who is used by him to explore the attitudes and reactions to the rapidly changing world of the later part of the nineteenth century, when transatlantic travel for middle-class American tourists was first becoming a possibility. Daisy Miller's freshness, innocence, audacity, candour, spontaneity and naïvety are cleverly contrasted with the complexity, stiffness and moral deviousness of not just the old staid European order, but of the well-established American community living there who have contrived to become more European than the Europeans. The book enjoyed great popularity and a *succès de scandale* on its publication and was instrumental in establishing Henry James's reputation on both sides of the Atlantic. The other stories in this collection are: *Four Meetings*, *Longstaff's Marriage* and *Benvolio*.

Henry James was born on 15 April 1843 at 21 Washington Place, New York City. His family was descended from English, Irish and Scottish Protestant stock who had emigrated to America and settled along the Hudson River. Indeed there is a street in Albany NY named after Henry James's Irish grandfather, William. William James achieved great commercial success, with the result that his son, Henry, the novelist's father, and Henry James himself could contemplate a life of literary ease almost unimaginable today. Henry James (senior) was a strong individualist, and his children's early lives were spent in a happy and seemingly never-ending peregrination from hotel to hotel, from school to school (Geneva, London, Paris and Boulogne-sur-mer) and from country to country (England, France and

Switzerland). Thus unconventional individualism was passed from one generation to the next in a youth that, while not an ideal training for some professions, could scarcely have been better suited to that of an incipient writer. Henry was also devoted to his mother, 'the keystone of the arch', his brother William, who was a philosopher, and his many cousins. He spent a term at Harvard Law School (1862/3) and then embarked on his writing career while continuing to travel to, from, and extensively within Europe. His work began to appear in the North American Review, *the* Nation, *and the* Atlantic Monthly. *In 1875 James left America to live in Paris where he met Ivan Turgenev, Gustave Flaubert, Émile Zola, Alphonse Daudet, Guy de Maupassant and Edmond de Goncourt. The following year he moved to London where he lived at 3 Bolton Street, Piccadilly. In 1878/9* Daisy Miller *and* The Europeans *were published, firmly establishing his reputation on both sides of the Atlantic. He was very much at home in London which he called 'the most complete compendium in the world'. In 1898 he moved to Lamb House, Rye, Sussex. Henry James's literary output was prodigious – twenty novels, innumerable stories including the well-known ghost story,* The Turn of the Screw *(1898), two biographies, many works of criticism or description, a number of plays, and two excellent pieces of autobiography. To each and every one of these he devoted great care and methodical planning, and his passionate interest in the* comédie humaine *informed and moulded his characters. Henry James's strong espousal of the British cause in the First World War led to his naturalisation as a British subject in 1915. He was awarded the Order of Merit in January 1916, and died on 28 February that year in Chelsea, London at the age of 72. His funeral was at Chelsea Old Church and his ashes are interred in the family plot in Cambridge, Massachusetts. A commemorative tablet was unveiled to him in Poets' Corner in Westminster Abbey on 17 June 1976.*

FURTHER READING

F. W. Dupee (ed.): *Autobiography* 1956 (reprinted 1983)
L. Edel: *The Life of Henry James* (revised edition 2 volumes 1977)
L. Edel (ed.): *Selected Letters of Henry James* 1955
F. O. Matthiessen and K. B. Murdock (eds): *The Notebook of Henry James* 1947 (reprinted 1981)
W. T. Stafford (ed.): *James's Daisy Miller* 1963

CONTENTS

DAISY MILLER
and other stories

Chapter 1

AT THE LITTLE TOWN of Vevey, in Switzerland, there is a particularly comfortable hotel. There are, indeed, many hotels; for the entertainment of tourists is the business of the place, which, as many travellers will remember, is seated upon the edge of a remarkably blue lake – a lake that it behoves every tourist to visit. The shore of the lake presents an unbroken array of establishments of this order, of every category, from the 'grand hotel' of the newest fashion, with a chalk-white front, a hundred balconies, and a dozen flags flying from its roof, to the little Swiss *pension* of an elder day, with its name inscribed in German-looking lettering upon a pink or yellow wall, and an awkward summer-house in the angle of the garden. One of the hotels at Vevey, however, is famous, even classical, being distinguished from many of its upstart neighbours by an air both of luxury and of maturity. In this region, in the month of June, American travellers are extremely numerous, it may be said indeed, that Vevey assumes at this period some of the characteristics of an American watering-place. There are sights and sounds which evoke a vision, an echo, of Newport and Saratoga. There is a flitting hither and thither of 'stylish' young girls, a rustling of muslin flounces, a rattle of dance music in the morning hours, a sound of high-pitched voices at all times. You receive an impression of these things at the excellent inn of the 'Trois Couronnes,' and are transported in fancy to the Ocean House or to Congress Hall. But at the 'Trois Couronnes,' it must be added, there are other features that are much at variance with these suggestions: neat German waiters, who look like secretaries of legation: Russian princesses sitting in the garden; little Polish boys walking about, held by the hand, with their governors; a view of the snowy crest of the Dent du Midi and the picturesque towers of the Castle of Chillon.

I hardly know whether it was the analogies or the differences that were uppermost in the mind of a young American, who, two or three years ago, sat in the garden of the 'Trois Couronnes,' looking about him, rather idly, at some of the graceful objects I have mentioned. It was a beautiful summer morning, and in whatever fashion the young American looked at things, they must have seemed to him charming.

He had come from Geneva the day before, by the little steamer, to see his aunt, who was staying at the hotel – Geneva having been for a long time his place of residence. But his aunt had a headache – his aunt had almost always a headache – and now she was shut up in her room, smelling camphor, so that he was at liberty to wander about. He was some seven-and-twenty years of age; when his friends spoke of him, they usually said that he was at Geneva, 'studying.' When his enemies spoke of him they said – but, after all, he had no enemies; he was an extremely amiable fellow, and universally liked. What I should say is, simply, that when certain persons spoke of him they affirmed that the reason of his spending so much time at Geneva was that he was extremely devoted to a lady who lived there – a foreign lady – a person older than himself. Very few Americans – indeed I think none – had ever seen this lady, about whom there were some singular stories. But Winterbourne had an old attachment for the little metropolis of Calvinism; he had been put to school there as a boy, and he had afterwards gone to college there – circumstances which had led to his forming a great many youthful friendships. Many of these he had kept, and they were a source of great satisfaction to him.

After knocking at his aunt's door and learning that she was indisposed, he had taken a walk about the town and then he had come in to his breakfast. He had now finished his breakfast, but he was drinking a small cup of coffee, which had been served to him on a little table in the garden by one of the waiters, who looked like an *attaché*. At last he finished his coffee and lit a cigarette. Presently a small boy came walking along the path – an urchin of nine or ten. The child, who was diminutive for his years, had an aged expression of countenance, a pale complexion, and sharp little features. He was dressed in knickerbockers, with red stockings, which displayed his poor little spindleshanks; he also wore a brilliant red cravat. He carried in his hand a long alpenstock, the sharp point of which he thrust into everything that he approached – the flower-beds, the garden benches, the trains of the ladies' dresses. In front of Winterbourne he paused, looking at him with a pair of bright penetrating little eyes.

'Will you give me a lump of sugar?' he asked, in a sharp hard little voice – a voice immature, and yet, somehow, not young.

Winterbourne glanced at the small table near him, on which his coffee-service rested, and saw that several morsels of sugar remained. 'Yes, you may take one,' he answered; 'but I don't think sugar is good for little boys.'

This little boy stepped forward and carefully selected three of the coveted fragments, two of which he buried in the pocket of his knickerbockers, depositing the other as promptly in another place. He poked his alpenstock, lance-fashion, into Winterbourne's bench, and tried to crack the lump of sugar with his teeth.

'Oh, blazes; it's har-r-d!' he exclaimed, pronouncing the adjective in a peculiar manner.

Winterbourne had immediately perceived that he might have the honour of claiming him as a fellow-countryman. 'Take care you don't hurt your teeth,' he said, paternally.

'I haven't got any teeth to hurt. They have all come out. I have only got seven teeth. My mother counted them last night, and one came out right afterwards. She said she'd slap me if any more came out. I can't help it. It's this old Europe. It's the climate that makes them come out. In America they didn't come out. It's these hotels.'

Winterbourne was much amused. 'If you eat three lumps of sugar your mother will certainly slap you,' he said.

'She's got to give me some candy, then,' rejoined his young interlocutor. 'I can't get any candy here – any American candy. American candy's the best candy.'

'And are American little boys the best little boys?' asked Winterbourne.

'I don't know. I'm an American boy,' said the child.

'I see you are one of the best!' laughed Winterbourne.

'Are you an American man?' pursued this vivacious infant. And then, on Winterbourne's affirmative reply – 'American men are the best,' he declared.

His companion thanked him for the compliment; and the child, who had now got astride of his alpenstock, stood looking about him, while he attacked a second lump of sugar. Winterbourne wondered if he himself had been like this in his infancy, for he had been brought to Europe at about this age.

'Here comes my sister!' cried the child, in a moment. 'She's an American girl.'

Winterbourne looked along the path and saw a beautiful young lady advancing. 'American girls are the best girls,' he said, cheerfully, to his young companion.

'My sister ain't the best!' the child declared. 'She's always blowing at me.'

'I imagine that is your fault, not hers,' said Winterbourne. The young lady meanwhile had drawn near. She was dressed in white muslin, with a hundred frills and flounces, and knots of pale-coloured ribbon. She was bare-headed; but she balanced in her hand a large parasol, with a deep border of embroidery; and she was strikingly, admirably pretty. 'How pretty they are!' thought Winterbourne, straightening himself in his seat, as if he were prepared to rise.

The young lady paused in front of his bench, near the parapet of the garden, which overlooked the lake. The little boy had now converted his alpenstock into a vaulting-pole, by the aid of which he was springing about in the gravel, and kicking it up not a little.

'Randolph,' said the young lady, 'what *are* you doing?'

'I'm going up the Alps,' replied Randolph. 'This is the way!' And he gave another little jump, scattering the pebbles about Winterbourne's ears.

'That's the way they come down,' said Winterbourne.

'He's an American man!' cried Randolph, in his little hard voice.

The young lady gave no heed to this announcement, but looked straight at her brother. 'Well, I guess you had better be quiet,' she simply observed.

It seemed to Winterbourne that he had been in a manner presented. He got up and stepped slowly towards the young girl, throwing away his cigarette. 'This little boy and I have made acquaintance,' he said, with great civility. In Geneva, as he had been perfectly aware, a young man was not at liberty to speak to a young unmarried lady except under certain rarely occurring conditions; but here at Vevey, what conditions could be better than these? – a pretty American girl coming and standing in front of you in a garden. This pretty American girl, however, on hearing Winterbourne's observation, simply glanced at him; she then turned her head and looked over the parapet, at the lake and the opposite mountains. He wondered whether he had gone too far; but he decided that he must advance farther, rather than retreat. While he was thinking of something else to say, the young lady turned to the little boy again.

'I should like to know where you got that pole,' she said.

'I bought it!' responded Randolph.

'You don't mean to say you're going to take it to Italy!'

'Yes, I am going to take it to Italy!' the child declared.

The young girl glanced over the front of her dress and smoothed out a knot or two of ribbon. Then she rested her eyes upon the prospect again. 'Well, I guess you had better leave it somewhere,' she said, after a moment.

'Are you going to Italy?' Winterbourne inquired, in a tone of great respect.

The young lady glanced at him again. 'Yes, sir,' she replied. And she said nothing more.

'Are you – a – going over the Simplon?' Winterbourne pursued, a little embarrassed.

'I don't know,' she said. 'I suppose it's some mountain. Randolph, what mountain are we going over?'

'Going where?' the child demanded.

'To Italy,' Winterbourne explained.

'I don't know,' said Randolph. 'I don't want to go to Italy. I want to go to America.'

'Oh, Italy is a beautiful place!' rejoined the young man.

'Can you get candy there?' Randolph loudly inquired.

'I hope not,' said his sister. 'I guess you have had enough candy, and mother thinks so too.'

'I haven't had any for ever so long – for a hundred weeks!' cried the boy, still jumping about.

The young lady inspected her flounces and smoothed her ribbons again; and Winterbourne presently risked an observation upon the beauty of the view. He was ceasing to be embarrassed, for he had begun to perceive that she was not in the least embarrassed herself. There had not been the slightest alteration in her charming complexion; she was evidently neither offended nor fluttered. If she looked another way when he spoke to her, and seemed not particularly to hear him, this was simply her habit, her manner. Yet, as he talked a little more, and pointed out some of the objects of interest in the view, with which she appeared quite unacquainted, she gradually gave him more of the benefit of her glance; and then he saw that this glance was perfectly direct and unshrinking. It was not, however, what would have been called an immodest glance, for the young girl's eyes were singularly honest and fresh. They were wonderfully pretty eyes; and, indeed, Winterbourne had not seen for a long time anything prettier than his fair countrywoman's various features – her complexion, her nose, her ears, her teeth. He had a great relish for feminine beauty; he was addicted to observing and analysing it; and as regards this young lady's face he made several observations. It was not at all insipid, but it was not exactly expressive; and though it was eminently delicate, Winterbourne mentally accused it – very forgivingly – of a want of finish. He thought it very possible that Master Randolph's sister was a coquette; he was sure she had a spirit of her own, but in her bright, sweet, superficial little visage, there was no mockery, no irony. Before long it became obvious that she was much disposed towards conversation. She told him that they were going to Rome for the winter – she and her mother and Randolph. She asked him if he was a 'real American;' she wouldn't have taken him for one, he seemed more like a German – this was said after a little hesitation – especially when he spoke. Winterbourne, laughing, answered that he had met Germans who spoke like Americans; but that he had not, so far as he remembered, met an American who spoke like a German. Then he asked her if she would not be more comfortable in sitting upon the bench which he had just quitted. She answered that she liked standing up and walking about; but she presently sat down. She told him she was from New York State – 'if you know where that is.' Winterbourne learned more about her by catching hold of her small slippery brother and making him stand a few minutes by his side.

'Tell me your name, my boy,' he said.

'Randolph C. Miller,' said the boy, sharply. 'And I'll tell you her name;' and he levelled his alpenstock at his sister.

'You had better wait till you are asked!' said this young lady, calmly.

'I should like very much to know your name,' said Winterbourne.

'Her name is Daisy Miller!' cried the child. 'Put that isn't her real name, that isn't her name on her cards.'

'It's a pity you haven't got one of my cards!' said Miss Miller.

'Her real name is Annie P. Miller,' the boy went on.

'Ask him *his* name,' said his sister indicating Winterbourne.

But on this point Randolph seemed perfectly indifferent; he continued to supply information with regard to his own family. 'My father's name is Ezra B. Miller,' he announced. 'My father ain't in Europe; my father's in a better place than Europe.'

Winterbourne imagined for a moment that this was the manner in which the child had been taught to intimate that Mr Miller had been removed to the sphere of celestial rewards. But Randolph immediately added, 'My father's in Schenectady. He's got a big business. My father's rich, you bet.'

'Well!' ejaculated Miss Miller, loweling her parasol and looking at the embroidered border. Winterbourne presently released the child, who departed, dragging his alpenstock along the path. 'He doesn't like Europe,' said the young girl. 'He wants to go back.'

'To Schenectady, you mean?'

'Yes; he wants to go right home. He hasn't got any boys here. There is one boy here, but he always goes round with a teacher; they won't let him play.'

'And your brother hasn't any teacher?' Winterbourne inquired.

'Mother thought of getting him one, to travel round with us. There was a lady told her of a very good teacher; an American lady – perhaps you know her – Mrs Sanders. I think she came from Boston. She told her of this teacher, and we thought of getting him to travel round with us. But Randolph said he didn't want a teacher travelling round with us. He said he wouldn't have lessons when he was in the cars. And we were in the cars about half the time. There was an English lady we met in the cars – I think her name was Miss Featherstone; perhaps you know her. She wanted to know why I didn't give Randolph lessons – give him "instruction," she called it. I guess he could give me more instruction than I could give him. He's very smart.'

'Yes,' said Winterbourne; 'he seems very smart.'

'Mother's going to get a teacher for him as soon as we get to Italy. Can you get good teachers in Italy?'

'Very good, I should think,' said Winterbourne.

'Or else she's going to find some school. He ought to learn some more. He's only nine. He's going to college.' And in this way Miss Miller continued to converse upon the affairs of her family, and upon other topics. She sat there with her extremely pretty hands, ornamented with very brilliant rings, folded in her lap, and with her pretty eyes now resting upon those of Winterbourne, now wandering over the garden, the people who passed by, and the beautiful view. She talked to Winterbourne as if she had known him a long time. He found it very pleasant. It was many years since he had heard a young girl talk so much. It might have been said of this unknown young lady, who had come and sat down beside him upon a bench, that she chattered. She was very quiet, she sat in a charming tranquil attitude; but her lips and her eyes were constantly moving. She had a soft, slender, agreeable voice, and her tone was decidedly sociable. She gave Winterbourne a history of her movements and intentions, and those of her mother and brother, in Europe, and enumerated, in particular, the various hotels at which they had stopped. 'That English lady in the cars,' she said – 'Miss Featherstone – asked me if we didn't all live in hotels in America. I told her I had never been in so many hotels in my life as since I came to Europe. I have never seen so many – it's nothing but hotels.' But Miss Miller did not make this remark with a querulous accent, she appeared to be in the best humour with everything. She declared that the hotels were very good, when once you got used to their ways, and that Europe was perfectly sweet. She was not disappointed – not a bit. Perhaps it was because she had heard so much about it before. She had ever so many intimate friends that had been there ever so many times.

And then she had had ever so many dresses and things from Paris. Whenever she put on a Paris dress she felt as if she were in Europe.

'It was a kind of a wishing-cap,' said Winterbourne.

'Yes,' said Miss Miller, without examining this analogy; 'it always made me wish I was here. But I needn't have done that for dresses. I am sure they send all the pretty ones to America; you see the most frightful things here. The only thing I don't like,' she proceeded, 'is the society. There isn't any society; or, if there is, I don't know where it keeps itself Do you? I suppose there is some society somewhere, but I haven't seen anything of it. I'm very fond of society, and I have always had a great deal of it. I don't mean only in Schenectady, but in New York. I used to go to New York every winter. In New York I had lots of society. Last winter I had seventeen dinners given me; and three of them were by gentlemen,' added Daisy Miller. 'I have more friends in New York than in Schenectady – more gentlemen friends; and more young lady friends too,' she resumed in a moment. She paused again for an instant- she was looking at Winterbourne with all her prettiness in her lively eyes and in her light, slightly monotonous smile. 'I have always had,' she said, 'a great deal of gentlemen's society.'

Poor Winterbourne was amused, perplexed, and decidedly charmed. He had never yet heard a young girl express herself in just this fashion; never, at least, save in cases where to say such things seemed a kind of demonstrative evidence of a certain laxity of deportment. And yet was he to accuse Miss Daisy Miller of actual or potential *inconduite*, as they said at Geneva? He felt that he had lived at Geneva so long that he had lost a good deal; he had become dishabituated to the American tone. Never indeed, since he had grown old enough to appreciate things, had he encountered a young American girl of so pronounced a type as this. Certainly she was very charming; but how deucedly sociable! Was she simply a pretty girl from New York State – were they all like that, the pretty girls who had a good deal of gentlemen's society? Or was she also a designing, an audacious, an unscrupulous young person? Winterbourne had lost his instinct in this matter, and his reason could not help him. Miss Daisy Miller looked extremely innocent. Some people had told him that, after all, American girls were exceedingly innocent; and others had told him that, after all, they were not. He was inclined to think Miss Daisy Miller was a flirt– a pretty American flirt. He had never, as yet, had any relations with young ladies of this category. He had known, here in Europe, two or three women – persons older than Miss Daisy Miller, and provided, for respectability's sake, with husbands – who were great coquettes – dangerous, terrible women, with whom one's relations were liable to take a serious turn. But this young girl was not a coquette in that sense; she was very unsophisticated; she was only a pretty American flirt. Winterbourne was almost grateful for having found the formula that applied to Miss Daisy Miller. He leaned back in his seat; he remarked to himself that she had the most charming nose he had ever seen; he wondered what were the regular conditions and limitations of one's intercourse with a pretty American flirt. It presently became apparent that he was on the way to learn.

'Have you been to that old castle?' asked the young girl, pointing with her parasol to the far-gleaming walls of the Château de Chillon.

'Yes, formerly, more than once,' said Winterbourne. 'You too, I suppose, have seen it?'

'No; we haven't been there. I want to go there dreadfully. Of course I mean to go there. I wouldn't go away from here without having seen that old castle.'

'It's a very pretty excursion,' said Winterbourne, 'and very easy to make. You can drive, you know, or you can go by the little steamer.'

'You can go in the cars,' said Miss Miller.

'Yes; you can go in the cars,' Winterbourne assented.

'Our courier says they take you right up to the castle,' the young girl continued. 'We were going last week; but my mother gave out. She suffers dreadfully from dyspepsia. She said she couldn't go. Randolph wouldn't go either; he says he doesn't think much of old castles. But I guess we'll go this week, if we can get Randolph.'

'Your brother is not interested in ancient monuments?' Winterbourne inquired, smiling.

'He says he don't care much about old castles. He's only nine. He wants to stay at the hotel. Mother's afraid to leave him alone, and the courier won't stay with him; so we haven't been to many places. But it will be too bad if we don't go up there.' And Miss Miller pointed again at the Château de Chillon.

'I should think it might be arranged,' said Winterbourne. 'Couldn't you get some one to stay – for the afternoon – with Randolph?'

Miss Miller looked at him a moment; and then, very placidly – 'I wish *you* would stay with him!' she said.

Winterbourne hesitated a moment. 'I would much rather go to Chillon with you.'

'With me?' asked the young girl, with the same placidity.

She didn't rise, blushing, as a young girl at Geneva would have done; and yet Winterbourne, conscious that he had been very bold, thought it possible she was offended. 'With your mother,' he answered very respectfully.

But it seemed that both his audacity and his respect were lost upon Miss Daisy Miller. 'I guess my mother won't go, after all,' she said. 'She don't like to ride round in the afternoon. But did you really mean what you said just now; that you would like to go up there?'

'Most earnestly,' Winterbourne declared.

'Then we may arrange it. If mother will stay with Randolph, I guess Eugenio will.'

'Eugenio?' the young man inquired

'Eugenio's our courier. He doesn't like to stay with Randolph; he's the most fastidious man I ever saw. But he's a splendid courier. I guess he'll stay at home with Randolph if mother does, and then we can go to the castle.'

Winterbourne reflected for an instant as lucidly as possible – 'we' could only mean Miss Daisy Miller and himself. This programme seemed almost too agreeable for credence; he felt as if he ought to kiss the young lady's hand. Possibly he would have done so – and quite spoiled the project; but at this moment another person – presumably Eugenio – appeared. A tall, handsome man, with superb whiskers, wearing a velvet morning coat and a brilliant watch-chain, approached Miss Miller, looking sharply at her companion. 'Oh, Eugenio!' said Miss Miller, with the friendliest accent.

Eugenio had looked at Winterbourne from head to foot; he now bowed gravely to the young lady. 'I have the honour to inform Mademoiselle that luncheon is upon the table.'

Miss Miller slowly rose. 'See here, Eugenio,' she said. 'I'm going to that old castle, anyway.'

'To the Château de Chillon Mademoiselle?' the courier inquired. 'Mademoiselle has made arrangements?' he added, in a tone which struck Winterbourne as very impertinent.

Eugenio's tone apparently threw, even to Miss Miller's own apprehension, a slightly ironical light upon the young girl's situation. She turned to Winterbourne blushing a little – a very little. 'You won't back out?' she said.

'I shall not be happy till we go!' he protested.

'And you are staying in this hotel?' she went on. 'And you are really an American?'

The courier stood looking at Winterbourne, offensively. The young man, at least, thought his manner of looking an offence to Miss Miller; it conveyed an imputation that she 'picked up' acquaintances. 'I shall have the honour of presenting to you a person who will tell you all about me,' he said, smiling, and referring to his aunt.

'Oh, well, we'll go some day,' said Miss Miller. And she gave him a smile and turned away. She put up her parasol and walked back to the inn beside Eugenio. Winterbourne stood looking after her; and as she moved away, drawing her muslin furbelows over the gravel, said to himself that she had the *tournure* of a princess.

Chapter 2

HE HAD, HOWEVER, ENGAGED to do more than proved feasible in promising to present his aunt, Mrs Costello, to Miss Daisy Miller. As soon as the former lady had got better of her headache he waited upon her in her apartment; and, after the proper inquiries in regard to her health, he asked her if she had observed, in the hotel, an American family – a mamma, a daughter, and a little boy.

'And a courier?' said Mrs Costello. 'Oh yes, I have observed them. Seen them – heard them – and kept out of their way.' Mrs Costello was a widow with a fortune; a person of much distinction, who frequently intimated that, if she were not so dreadfully liable to sick-headaches, she would probably have left a deeper impress upon her time. She had a long pale face, a high nose, and a great deal of very striking white hair, which she wore in large puffs and *rouleaux* over the top of her head. She had two sons married in New York, and another who was now in Europe. This young man was amusing himself at Homburg, and, though he was on his travels, was rarely perceived to visit any particular city at the moment selected by his mother for her own appearance there. Her nephew who had come up to Vevey expressly to see her, was therefore more attentive than those who, as she said, were nearer to her. He had imbibed at Geneva the idea that one must always be attentive to one's aunt. Mrs Costello had not seen him for many years, and she was greatly pleased with him, manifesting her approbation by initiating him into many of the secrets of that social sway which, as she gave him to understand, she exerted in the American capital. She admitted that she was very exclusive, but, if he were acquainted with New York, he would see that one had to be. And her picture of the minutely hierarchical constitution of the society of that city, which she presented to him in many different lights, was, to Winterbourne's imagination, almost oppressively striking.

He immediately perceived, from her tone, that Miss Daisy Miller's place in the social scale was low. 'I am afraid you don't approve of them,' he said.

'They are very common,' Mrs Costello declared. 'They are the sort of Americans that one does one's duty by not – not accepting.'

'Ah, you don't accept them?' said the young man.

'I can't, my dear Frederick. I would if I could, but I can't.'

'The young girl is very pretty,' said Winterbourne, in a moment.

'Of course she's pretty. But she is very common.'

'I see what you mean, of course,' said Winterbourne, after another pause.

'She has that charming look they all have,' his aunt resumed. 'I can't think where they pick it up; and she dresses in perfection – no, you don't know how well she dresses. I can't think where they get their taste.'

'But, my dear aunt, she is not, after all, a Comanche savage.'

'She is a young lady,' said Mrs Costello, 'who has an intimacy with her mamma's courier!'

'An intimacy with the courier?' the young man demanded.

'Oh, the mother is just as bad! They treat the courier like a familiar friend – like a gentleman. I shouldn't wonder if he dines with them. Very likely they have never seen a man with such good manners, such fine clothes, so like a gentleman. He probably corresponds to the young lady's idea of a count. He sits with them in the garden, in the evening. I think he smokes.'

Winterbourne listened with interest to these disclosures; they helped him to make up his mind about Miss Daisy. Evidently she was rather wild. 'Well,' he said, 'I am not a courier, and yet she was very charming to me.'

'You had better have said at first,' said Mrs Costello with dignity, 'that you had made her acquaintance.'

'We simply met in the garden, and we talked a bit.'

'*Tout bonnement!* And pray what did you say?'

'I said I should take the liberty of introducing her to my admirable aunt.'

'I am much obliged to you.'

'It was to guarantee my respectability,' said Winterbourne.

'And pray who is to guarantee hers?'

'Ah, you are cruel!' said the young man. 'She's a very nice girl.'

'You don't say that as if you believed it,' Mrs Costello observed.

'She is completely uncultivated,' Winterbourne went on. 'But she is wonderfully pretty, and, in short, she is very nice. To prove that I believe it, I am going to take her to the Château de Chillon.'

'You two are going off there together? I should say it proved just the contrary. How long had you known her, may I ask, when this interesting project was formed? You haven't been twenty-four hours in the house.'

'I had known her half an hour!' said Winterbourne smiling

'Dear me!' cried Mrs Costello. 'What a dreadful girl!'

Her nephew was silent for some moments. 'You really think, then,' he began earnestly, and with a desire for trustworthy information – 'you really think that – ' But he paused again.

'Think what, sir?' said his aunt.

'That she is the sort of young lady who expects a man – sooner or later – to carry her off?'

'I haven't the least idea what such young ladies expect a man to do. But I really think that you had better not meddle with little American girls that are uncultivated, as you call them. You have lived too long out of the country. You will be sure to make some great mistake. You are too innocent.'

'My dear aunt, I am not so innocent,' said Winterbourne, smiling and curling his moustache.

'You are too guilty, then!'

Winterbourne continued to curl his moustache, meditatively. 'You won't let the poor girl know you, then?' he asked at last.

'Is it literally true that she is going to the Château de Chillon with you?'

'I think that she fully intends it.'

'Then, my dear Frederick,' said Mrs Costello, 'I must decline the honour of her acquaintance. I am an old woman, but I am not too old – thank Heaven – to be shocked!'

'But don't they all do these things – the young girls in America?' Winterbourne inquired.

Mrs Costello stared a moment. 'I should like to see my granddaughters do them!' she declared, grimly.

This seemed to throw some light upon the matter, for Winterbourne remembered to have heard that his pretty cousins in New York were 'tremendous flirts.' If, therefore, Miss Daisy Miller exceeded the liberal license allowed to these young ladies, it was probable that anything might be expected of her. Winterbourne was impatient to see her again, and he was vexed with himself that, by instinct, he should not appreciate her justly.

Though he was impatient to see her, he hardly knew what he should say to her about his aunt's refusal to become acquainted with her, but he discovered, promptly enough, that with Miss Daisy Miller there was no great need of walking on tiptoe. He found her that evening in the garden, wandering about in the warm starlight, like an indolent sylph, and swinging to and fro the largest fan he had ever beheld. It was ten o'clock. He had dined with his aunt, had been sitting with her since dinner, and had just taken leave of her till the morrow. Miss Daisy Miller seemed very glad to see him; she declared it was the longest evening she had ever passed

'Have you been all alone?' he asked.

'I have been walking round with mother. But mother gets tired walking round,' she answered.

'Has she gone to bed?'

'No; she doesn't like to go to bed,' said the young girl. 'She doesn't sleep – not three hours. She says she doesn't know how she lives. She's dreadfully nervous. I guess she sleeps more than she thinks. She's gone somewhere after Randolph; she wants to try to get him to go to bed. He doesn't like to go to bed.'

'Let us hope she will persuade him,' observed Winterbourne.

'She will talk to him all she can; but he doesn't like her to talk to him,' said Miss Daisy, opening her fan. 'She's going to try to get Eugenio to talk to him. But he isn't afraid of Eugenio. Eugenio's a splendid courier, but he can't make much impression on Randolph! I don't believe he'll go to bed before eleven.' It appeared that Randolph's vigil was in fact triumphantly prolonged, for Winterbourne strolled about with the young girl for some time without meeting her mother. 'I have been looking round for that lady you want to introduce me to,' his companion resumed. 'She's your aunt.' Then on Winterbourne's admitting the fact, and expressing some curiosity as to how she had learned it, she said she had heard all about Mrs Costello from the chamber maid. She was very quiet and very *comme il faut*; she wore white puffs; she spoke to no one, and she never dined at the *table d'hôte*. Every two days she had a headache. 'I think that's a lovely description, headache and all!' said Miss Daisy, chattering along in her thin, gay voice. 'I want to know her ever so much. I know just what *your* aunt would be; I know I should like her. She would be very exclusive. I like a lady to be exclusive; I'm dying to be exclusive myself. Well, we *are* exclusive, mother and I. We don't speak to every one – or they don't speak to us. I suppose it's about the same thing. Any way, I shall be ever so glad to know your aunt.'

Winterbourne was embarrassed. 'She would be most happy,' he said;

'but I am afraid those headaches will interfere.'

The young girl looked at him through the dusk. 'But I suppose she doesn't have a headache every day,' she said, sympathetically.

Winterbourne was silent a moment. 'She tells me she does,' he answered at last – not knowing what to say.

Miss Daisy Miller stopped and stood looking at him.

Her prettiness was still visible in the darkness; she was opening and closing her enormous fan. 'She doesn't want to know me!' she said, suddenly. 'Why don't you say so? You needn't be afraid. I'm not afraid!' And she gave a little laugh.

Winterbourne fancied there was a tremor in her voice; he was touched, shocked, mortified by it. 'My dear young lady,' he protested, 'she knows no one. It's her wretched health.'

The young girl walked on a few steps, laughing still. 'You needn't be afraid,' she repeated. 'Why should she want to know me?' Then she paused again; she was close to the parapet of the garden, and in front of her was the starlit lake. There was a vague sheen upon its surface, and in the distance were dimly-seen mountain forms. Daisy Miller looked out upon the mysterious prospect, and then she gave another little laugh. 'Gracious! she *is* exclusive!' she said. Winterbourne wondered whether she was seriously wounded, and for a moment almost wished that her sense of injury might be such as to make it becoming in him to attempt to reassure and comfort her. He had a pleasant sense that she would be very approachable for consolatory purposes. He felt then, for the instant, quite ready to sacrifice his aunt, conversationally; to admit that she was a proud, rude woman, and to declare that they needn't mind her. But before he had time to commit himself to this perilous mixture of gallantry and impiety, the young lady, resuming her walk, gave an exclamation in quite another tone. 'Well; here's mother! I guess she hasn't got Randolph to go to bed.' The figure of a lady appeared, at a distance, very indistinct in the darkness, and advancing with a slow and wavering movement. Suddenly it seemed to pause.

'Are you sure it is your mother? Can you distinguish her in this thick dusk?' Winterbourne asked.

'Well!' cried Miss Daisy Miller, with a laugh, 'I guess I know my own mother. And when she has got on my shawl, too! She is always wearing my things.'

The lady in question, ceasing to advance, hovered vaguely about the spot at which she had checked her steps.

'I am afraid your mother doesn't see you,' said Winterbourne. 'Or perhaps,' he added – thinking, with Miss Miller, the joke permissible –

'perhaps she feels guilty about your shawl.'

'Oh, it's a fearful old thing!' the young girl replied, serenely. 'I told her she could wear it. She won't come here, because she sees you.'

'Ah, then,' said Winterbourne, 'I had better leave you.'

'Oh no! come on!' urged Miss Daisy Miller.

'I'm afraid your mother doesn't approve of my walking with you.'

Miss Miller gave him a serious glance. 'It isn't for me; it's for you – that is, it's for *her*. Well, I don't know who it's for! But mother doesn't like any of my gentlemen friends. She's right down timid. She always makes a fuss if I introduce a gentleman. But I *do* introduce them – almost always. If I didn't introduce my gentlemen friends to mother,' the young girl added, in her little soft, flat monotone, 'I shouldn't think I was natural.'

'To introduce me,' said Winterbourne, 'you must know my name.' And he proceeded to pronounce it.

'Oh dear; I can't say all that!' said his companion with a laugh. But by this time they had come up to Mrs Miller, who, as they drew near, walked to the parapet of the garden and leaned upon it, looking intently at the lake and turning her back upon them. 'Mother!' said the young girl in a tone of decision. Upon this the elder lady turned round. 'Mr Winterbourne,' said Miss Daisy Miller, introducing the young man very frankly and prettily. 'Common' she was, as Mrs Costello had pronounced her; yet it was a wonder to Winterbourne that, with her commonness, she had a singularly delicate grace.

Her mother was a small, spare, light person, with a wandering eye, a very exiguous nose, and a large forehead, decorated with a certain amount of thin, much frizzled hair. Like her daughter, Mrs Miller was dressed with extreme elegance: she had enormous diamonds in her ears. So far as Winterbourne could observe, she gave him no greeting – she certainly was not looking at him. Daisy was near her, pulling her shawl straight. 'What are you doing, poking round here?' this young lady inquired; but by no means with that harshness of accent which her choice of words may imply.

'I don't know,' said her mother, turning towards the lake again.

'I shouldn't think you'd want that shawl!' Daisy exclaimed.

'Well – I do!' her mother answered, with a little laugh.

'Did you get Randolph to go to bed?' asked the young girl.

'No; I couldn't induce him,' said Mrs Miller, very gently. 'He wants to talk to the waiter. He likes to talk to that waiter.'

'I was telling Mr Winterbourne,' the young girl went on; and to the young man's ear her tone might have indicated that she had been uttering his name all her life.

'Oh yes!' said Winterbourne; 'I have the pleasure of knowing your son.'

Randolph's mamma was silent; she turned her attention to the lake. But at last she spoke. 'Well, I don't see how he lives!'

'Anyhow, it isn't so bad as it was at Dover,' said Daisy Miller.

'And what occurred at Dover?' Winterbourne asked.

'He wouldn't go to bed at all. I guess he sat up all night – in the public parlour. He wasn't in bed at twelve o'clock: I know that.'

'It was half-past twelve,' declared Mrs Miller, with mild emphasis.

'Does he sleep much during the day?' Winterbourne demanded.

'I guess he doesn't sleep much,' Daisy rejoined.

'I wish he would!' said her mother. 'It seems as if he couldn't.'

'I think he's real tiresome,' Daisy pursued.

Then, for some moments, there was silence. 'Well, Daisy Miller,' said the elder lady, presently, 'I shouldn't think you'd want to talk against your own brother!'

'Well, he *is* tiresome, mother,' said Daisy, quite without the asperity of a retort.

'He's only nine,' urged Mrs Miller.

'Well, he wouldn't go to that castle,' said the young girl. 'I'm going there with Mr Winterbourne.'

To this announcement, very placidly made, Daisy's mamma offered no response. Winterbourne took for granted that she deeply disapproved of the projected excursion; but he said to himself that she was a simple, easily-managed person, and that a few deferential protestations would take the edge from her displeasure. 'Yes,' he began; 'your daughter has kindly allowed me the honour of being her guide.'

Mrs Miller's wandering eyes attached themselves, with a sort of appealing air, to Daisy, who, however, strolled a few steps farther, gently humming to herself. 'I presume you will go in the cars,' said her mother.

'Yes; or in the boat,' said Winterbourne.

'Well, of course, I don't know,' Mrs Miller rejoined. 'I have never been to that castle.'

'It is a pity you shouldn't go,' said Winterbourne beginning to feel reassured as to her opposition. And yet he was quite prepared to find that, as a matter of course, she meant to accompany her daughter.

'We've been thinking ever so much about going,' she pursued; 'but it seems as if we couldn't. Of course Daisy – she wants to go round. But there's a lady here – I don't know her name – she says she shouldn't think we'd want to go to see castles *here*; she should think we'd want to wait till we got to Italy. It seems as if there would be so many there,' continued Mrs Miller, with an air of increasing confidence. 'Of course, we only want to see the principal ones. We visited several in England,' she presently added.

'Ah yes! in England there are beautiful castles,' said Winterbourne. 'But Chillon, here, is very well worth seeing.'

'Well, if Daisy feels up to it – ' said Mrs Miller, in a tone impregnated with a sense of the magnitude of the enterprise. 'It seems as if there was nothing she wouldn't undertake.'

'Oh, I think she'll enjoy it!' Winterbourne declared. And he desired more and more to make it a certainty that he was to have the privilege of a *tête-à-tête* with the young lady, who was still strolling along in front of them, softly vocalising. 'You are not disposed, madam,' he inquired, 'to undertake it yourself?'

Daisy's mother looked at him an instant, askance, and then walked forward in silence. Then – 'I guess she had better go alone,' she said, simply.

Winterbourne observed to himself that this was a very different type of maternity from that of the vigilant matrons who massed themselves in the forefront of social intercourse in the dark old city at the other end of the lake. But his meditations were interrupted by hearing his name very distinctly pronounced by Mrs Miller's unprotected daughter.

'Mr Winterbourne!' murmured Daisy.

'Mademoiselle!' said the young man.

'Don't you want to take me out in a boat?'

'At present?' he asked.

'Of course!' said Daisy.

'Well, Annie Miller!' exclaimed her mother.

'I beg you, madam, to let her go,' said Winterbourne, ardently; for he had never yet enjoyed the sensation of guiding through the summer starlight a skiff freighted with a fresh and beautiful young girl.

'I shouldn't think she'd want to,' said her mother. 'I should think she'd rather go indoors.'

'I'm sure Mr Winterbourne wants to take me,' Daisy declared. 'He's so awfully devoted!'

'I will row you over to Chillon in the starlight.'

'I don't believe it!' said Daisy.

'Well!' ejaculated the elder lady again.

'You haven't spoken to me for half an hour,' her daughter went on.

'I have been having some very pleasant conversation with your mother,' said Winterbourne.

'Well; I want you to take me out in a boat!' Daisy repeated. They had all stopped, and she had turned round and was looking at Winterbourne. Her face wore a charming smile, her pretty eyes were gleaming, she was swinging her great fan about. No; it's impossible to be prettier than that, thought Winterbourne.

'There are half- a- dozen boats moored at that landing place,' he said, pointing to certain steps which descended from the garden to the lake. 'If you will do me the honour to accept my arm, we will go and select one of them.'

Daisy stood there smiling; she threw back her head and gave a little light laugh. 'I like a gentleman to be formal!' she declared.

'I assure you it's a formal offer.'

'I was bound I would make you say something,' Daisy went on.

'You see it's not very difficult,' said Winterbourne. 'But I am afraid you are charming me.'

'I think not, sir,' remarked Mrs Miller, very gently.

'Do, then, let me give you a row,' he said to the young girl.

'It's quite lovely, the way you say that!' cried Daisy.

'It will be still more lovely to do it.'

'Yes, it would be lovely!' said Daisy. But she made no movement to accompany him; she only stood there laughing

'I should think you had better find out what time it is,' interposed her mother.

'It is eleven o'clock, madam,' said a voice, with a foreign accent, out of the neighbouring darkness; and Winterbourne, turning, perceived the florid personage who was in attendance upon the two ladies. He had apparently just approached.

'Oh, Eugenio,' said Daisy, 'I am going out in a boat!'

Eugenio bowed. 'At eleven o'clock, Mademoiselle?'

'I am going with Mr Winterbourne. This very minute.'

'Do tell her she can't,' said Mrs Miller to the courier

'I think you had better not go out in a boat, Mademoiselle,' Eugenio declared.

Winterbourne wished to Heaven this pretty girl were not so familiar with her courier, but he said nothing.

'I suppose you don't think it's proper!' Daisy exclaimed. 'Eugenio doesn't think anything's proper.'

'I am at your service,' said Winterbourne.

'Does Mademoiselle propose to go alone?' asked Eugenio of Mrs Miller.

'Oh no; with this gentleman!' answered Daisy's mamma.

The courier looked for a moment at Winterbourne – the latter thought he was smiling – and then, solemnly, with a bow, 'As Mademoiselle pleases!' he said.

'Oh, I hoped you would make a fuss!' said Daisy. 'I don't care to go now.'

'I myself shall make a fuss if you don't go,' said Winterbourne.

'That's all I want – a little fuss!' And the young girl began to laugh again.

'Mr Randolph has gone to bed!' the courier announced, frigidly.

'Oh, Daisy; now we can go!' said Mrs Miller.

Daisy turned away from Winterbourne, looking at him, smiling and fanning herself. 'Good-night,' she said; 'I hope you are disappointed, or disgusted, or something!'

He looked at her, taking the hand she offered him. 'I am puzzled,' he answered.

'Well; I hope it won't keep you awake!' she said very smartly; and, under the escort of the privileged Eugenio, the two ladies passed towards the house.

Winterbourne stood looking after them, he was indeed puzzled. He lingered beside the lake for a quarter of an hour, turning over the mystery of the young girl's sudden familiarities and caprices. But the only very definite conclusion he came to was that he should enjoy deucedly 'going off' with her somewhere.

Two days afterwards he went off with her to the Castle of Chillon. He waited for her in the large hall of the hotel, where the couriers, the servants, the foreign tourists, were lounging about and staring. It was not the place he would have chosen, but she had appointed it. She came tripping downstairs, buttoning her long gloves, squeezing her folded parasol against her pretty figure, dressed in the perfection of a soberly elegant travelling costume. Winterbourne was a man of imagination and, as our ancestors used to say, of sensibility; as he looked at her dress and, on the great staircase, her little rapid, confiding step, he felt as if there were something romantic going forward. He could have believed he was going to elope with her. He passed out with her among all the idle people that were assembled there; they were all looking at her very hard; she had begun to chatter as soon as she joined him. Winterbourne's preference had been that they should be conveyed to Chillon in a carriage; but she expressed a lively wish to go in the little steamer; she declared that she had a passion for steamboats. There was always such a lovely breeze upon the water and you saw such lots of people.

The sail was not long, but Winterbourne's companion found time to say a great many things. To the young man himself their little excursion was so much of an escapade – an adventure – that, even allowing for her habitual sense of freedom, he had some expectation of seeing her regard it in the same way. But it must be confessed that, in this particular, he was disappointed. Daisy Miller was extremely animated, she was in charming spirits; but she was apparently not at all excited; she was not fluttered; she avoided neither his eyes nor those of any one else; she blushed neither when she looked at him nor when she saw that people were looking at her. People continued to look at her a great deal, and Winterbourne took much satisfaction in his pretty companion's distinguished air. He had been a little afraid that she would talk loud, laugh overmuch, and even, perhaps, desire to move about the boat a good deal. But he quite forgot his fears; he sat smiling, with his eyes upon her face, while, without moving from her place, she delivered herself of a great number of original reflections. It was the most charming garrulity he had ever heard. He had assented to the idea that she was 'common;' but was she so, after all, or was he simply getting used to her commonness? Her conversation was chiefly of what metaphysicians term the objective cast; but every now and then it took a subjective turn.

'What on *earth* are you so grave about?' she suddenly demanded, fixing her agreeable eyes upon Winterbourne's.

'Am I grave?' he asked. 'I had an idea I was grinning from ear to ear.'

'You look as if you were taking me to a funeral. If that's a grin, your ears are very near together.'

'Should you like me to dance a hornpipe on the deck?'

'Pray do, and I'll carry round your hat. It will pay the expenses of our journey.'

'I never was better pleased in my life,' murmured Winterbourne.

She looked at him a moment, and then burst into a little laugh. 'I like to make you say those things! You're a queer mixture!'

In the castle, after they had landed, the subjective element decidedly prevailed. Daisy tripped about the vaulted chambers, rustled her skirts in the corkscrew staircases, flirted back with a pretty little cry and a shudder from the edge of the *oubliettes*, and turned a singularly well-shaped ear to everything that Winterbourne told her about the place. But he saw that she cared very little for feudal antiquities, and that the dusky traditions of Chillon made but a slight impression upon her. They had the good fortune to have been able to walk about without other companionship than that of the custodian, and Winterbourne arranged with this functionary that they should not be hurried – that they should linger and pause wherever they chose. The custodian interpreted the bargain generously – Winterbourne, on his side, had been generous – and ended by leaving them quite to themselves. Miss Miller's observations were not remarkable for logical consistency; for anything she wanted to say she was sure to find a pretext. She found a great many pretexts in the rugged embrasures of Chillon for asking Winterbourne sudden questions about himself – his family, his previous history, his tastes, his habits, his intentions – and for supplying information upon corresponding points in her own personality. Of her own tastes, habits, and intentions Miss Miller was prepared to give the most definite, and indeed the most favourable, account.

'Well; I hope you know enough!' she said to her companion, after he had told her the history of the unhappy Bonivard. 'I never saw a man that knew so much!' The history of Bonivard had evidently, as they say, gone into one ear and out of the other. But Daisy went on to say that she wished Winterbourne would travel with them and 'go round' with them; they might know something, in that case. 'Don't you want to come and teach Randolph?' she asked. Winterbourne said that nothing could possibly please him so much; but that he had unfortunately other occupations. 'Other occupations? I don't believe it!' said Miss Daisy. 'What do you mean? You are not in business.' The young man admitted that he was not in business; but he had engagements which, even within a day or two, would force him to go back to Geneva. 'Oh, bother!' she said, 'I don't believe it!' and she began to talk about something else. But a few moments later, when he was pointing out to her the pretty design of an antique fireplace, she broke out irrelevantly, 'You don't mean to say you are going back to Geneva?'

'It is a melancholy fact that I shall have to return to Geneva tomorrow.'

'Well, Mr Winterbourne,' said Daisy; 'I think you're horrid!'

'Oh, don't say such dreadful things!' said Winterbourne – 'just at the last.'

'The last!' cried the young girl; 'I call it the first. I have half a mind to leave you here and go straight back to the hotel alone.' And for the next ten minutes she did nothing but call him horrid. Poor Winterbourne was fairly bewildered; no young lady had as yet done him the honour to be so agitated by the announcement of his movements. His companion after this, ceased to pay any attention to the curiosities of Chillon or the beauties of the lake; she opened fire upon the mysterious charmer in Geneva, whom she appeared to have instantly taken it for granted that he was hurrying back to see. How did Miss Daisy Miller know that there was a charmer in Geneva? Winterbourne, who denied the existence of such a person, was quite unable to discover; and he was divided between amazement at the rapidity of her induction and amusement at the frankness of her *persiflage*. She seemed to him, in all this, an extraordinary mixture of innocence and crudity. 'Does she never allow you more than three days at a time?' asked Daisy, ironically. 'Doesn't she give you a vacation in summer? There's no one so hard worked, but they can get leave to go off somewhere at this season. I suppose, if you stay another day, she'll come after you in the boat. Do wait over till Friday, and I will go down to the landing to see her arrive!' Winterbourne began to think he had been wrong to feel disappointed in the temper in which the young lady had embarked. If he had missed the personal accent, the personal accent was now making its appearance. It sounded very distinctly, at last, in her telling him she would stop 'teasing' him if he would promise her solemnly to come down to Rome in the winter.

'That's not a difficult promise to make,' said Winterbourne. 'My aunt has taken an apartment in Rome for the winter, and has already asked me to come and see her.'

'I don't want you to come for your aunt,' said Daisy; 'I want you to come for me.' And this was the only allusion that the young man was ever to hear her make to his invidious kinswoman. He declared that, at any rate, he would certainly come. After this Daisy stopped teasing. Winterbourne took a carriage, and they drove back to Vevey in the dusk; the young girl was very quiet.

In the evening Winterbourne mentioned to Mrs Costello that he had spent the afternoon at Chillon with Miss Daisy Miller.

'The Americans – of the courier?' asked this lady.

'Ah, happily,' said Winterbourne, 'the courier stayed at home.'

'She went with you all alone?'

'All alone.'

Mrs Costello sniffed a little at her smelling-bottle. 'And that,' she exclaimed, 'is the young person you wanted me to know!'

Chapter 3

WINTERBOURNE, who had returned to Geneva the day after his excursion to Chillon, went to Rome towards the end of January. His aunt had been established there for several weeks, and he had received a couple of letters from her. 'Those people you were so devoted to last summer at Vevey have turned up here, courier and all,' she wrote. 'They seem to have made several acquaintances, but the courier continues to be the most *intime*. The young lady, however, is also very intimate with some third-rate Italians, with whom she rackets about in a way that makes much talk. Bring me that pretty novel of Cherbuliez's – "Paule Méré" – and don't come later than the 23rd.'

In the natural course of events Winterbourne, on arriving in Rome, would presently have ascertained Mrs Miller's address at the American banker's, and have gone to pay his compliments to Miss Daisy. 'After what happened at Vevey I certainly think I may call upon them,' he said to Mrs Costello.

'If, after what happens – at Vevey and everywhere – you desire to keep up the acquaintance, you are very welcome. Of course a man may know every one. Men are welcome to the privilege!'

'Pray, what is it that happens – here, for instance?' Winterbourne demanded.

'The girl goes about alone with her foreigners. As to what happens farther, you must apply elsewhere for information. She has picked up half-a-dozen of the regular Roman fortune hunters, and she takes them about to people's houses. When she comes to a party she brings with her a gentleman with a good deal of manner and a wonderful moustache.'

'And where is the mother?'

'I haven't the least idea. They are very dreadful people.'

Winterbourne meditated a moment. 'They are very ignorant – very innocent only. Depend upon it they are not bad.'

'They are hopelessly vulgar,' said Mrs Costello. 'Whether or no being hopelessly vulgar is being "bad" is a question for the metaphysicians. They are bad enough to dislike, at any rate; and for this short life that is quite enough.'

The news that Daisy Miller was surrounded by half-a-dozen wonderful moustaches checked Winterbourne's impulse to go straightway to see her. He had perhaps not definitely flattered himself that he had made an ineffaceable impression upon her heart, but he was annoyed at hearing of a state of affairs so little in harmony with an image that had lately flitted in and out of his own meditations; the image of a very pretty girl looking out of an old Roman window and asking herself urgently when Mr Winterbourne would arrive. If, however, he determined to wait a little before reminding Miss Miller of his claims to her consideration, he went very soon to call upon two or three other friends. One of these friends was an American lady who had spent several winters at Geneva, where she had placed her children at school.

She was a very accomplished woman, and she lived in the Via Gregoriana. Winterbourne found her in a little crimson drawing-room, on a third floor; the room was filled with southern sunshine. He had not been there ten minutes when the servant came in, announcing 'Madame Mila!' This announcement was presently followed by the entrance of little Randolph Miller, who stopped in the middle of the room and stood staring at Winterbourne. An instant later his pretty sister crossed the threshold; and then, after a considerable interval, Mrs Miller slowly advanced.

'I know you!' said Randolph.

'I'm sure you know a great many things,' exclaimed Winterbourne, taking him by the hand. 'How is your education coming on?'

Daisy was exchanging greetings very prettily with her hostess; but when she heard Winterbourne's voice she quickly turned her head. 'Well, I declare!' she said.

'I told you I should come, you know,' Winterbourne rejoined smiling.

'Well – I didn't believe it,' said Miss Daisy.

'I am much obliged to you,' laughed the young man.

'You might have come to see me!' said Daisy.

'I arrived only yesterday.'

'I don't believe that!' the young girl declared.

Winterbourne turned with a protesting smile to her mother; but this lady evaded his glance, and seating herself, fixed her eyes upon her son. 'We've got a bigger place than this,' said Randolph. 'It's all gold on the walls.'

Mrs Miller turned uneasily in her chair. 'I told you if I were to bring you you would say something!' she murmured.

'I told *you*!' Randolph exclaimed. 'I tell *you*, sir!' he added jocosely, giving Winterbourne a thump on the knee. 'It is bigger, too!'

Daisy had entered upon a lively conversation with her hostess; Winterbourne judged it becoming to address a few words to her mother. 'I hope you have been well since we parted at Vevey,' he said.

Mrs Miller now certainly looked at him – at his chin. 'Not very well, sir,' she answered.

'She's got the dyspepsia,' said Randolph. 'I've got it too. Father's got it. I've got it worst!'

This announcement, instead of embarrassing Mrs Miller, seemed to relieve her. 'I suffer from the liver,' she said. 'I think it's this climate; it's less bracing than Schenectady, especially in the winter season. I don't know whether you know we reside at Schenectady. I was saying to Daisy that I certainly hadn't found any one like Dr Davis, and I didn't believe I should. Oh, at Schenectady, he stands first; they think everything of him. He has so much to do, and yet there was nothing he wouldn't do for me. He said he never saw anything like my dyspepsia, but he was bound to cure it. I'm sure there was nothing he wouldn't try. He was just going to try something new when we came off. Mr Miller wanted Daisy to see Europe for herself. But I wrote to Mr Miller that it seems as if I couldn't get on without Dr Davis. At Schenectady he stands at the very top; and there's a great deal of sickness there, too. It affects my sleep.'

Winterbourne had a good deal of pathological gossip with Dr Davis's patient, during which Daisy chattered unremittingly to her own companion. The young man asked Mrs Miller how she was pleased with Rome. 'Well, I must say I am disappointed,' she answered. 'We had heard so much about it; I suppose we had heard too much. But we couldn't help that. We had been led to expect something different.'

'Ah, wait a little, and you will become very fond of it,' said Winterbourne.

'I hate it worse and worse every day!' cried Randolph.

'You are like the infant Hannibal,' said Winterbourne.

'No, I ain't!' Randolph declared, at a venture.

'You are not much like an infant,' said his mother. 'But we have seen places,' she resumed, 'that I should put a long way before Rome.' And in reply to Winterbourne's interrogation, 'There's Zurich,' she observed; 'I think Zurich is lovely; and we hadn't heard half so much about it.'

'The best place we've seen is the City of Richmond!' said Randolph.

'He means the ship,' his mother explained. 'We crossed in that ship. Randolph had a good time on the City of Richmond.'

'It's the best place I've seen,' the child repeated. 'Only it was turned the wrong way.'

'Well, we've got to turn the right way some time,' said Mrs Miller, with a little laugh. Winterbourne expressed the hope that her daughter at least found some gratification in Rome, and she declared that Daisy was quite carried away. 'It's on account of the society – the society's splendid. She goes round everywhere, she has made a great number of acquaintances. Of course she goes round more than I do. I must say they have been very sociable; they have taken her right in. And then she knows a great many gentlemen. Oh, she thinks there's nothing like Rome. Of course, it's a great deal pleasanter for a young lady if she knows plenty of gentlemen.'

By this time Daisy had turned her attention again to Winterbourne. 'I've been telling Mrs Walker how mean you were!' the young girl announced.

'And what is the evidence you have offered?' asked Winterbourne, rather annoyed at Miss Miller's want of appreciation of the zeal of an admirer who on his way down to Rome had stopped neither at Bologna nor at Florence, simply because of a certain sentimental impatience. He remembered that a cynical compatriot had once told him that American women – the pretty ones and this gave a largeness to the axiom – were at once the most exacting in the world and the least endowed with a sense of indebtedness.

'Why, you were awfully mean at Vevey,' said Daisy. 'You wouldn't do anything. You wouldn't stay there when I asked you.'

'My dearest young lady,' cried Winterbourne, with eloquence, 'have I come all the way to Rome to encounter your reproaches?'

'Just hear him say that!' said Daisy to her hostess, giving a twist to a bow on this lady's dress. 'Did you ever hear anything so quaint?'

'So quaint, my dear?' murmured Mrs Walker, in the tone of a partisan of Winterbourne.

'Well, I don't know,' said Daisy, fingering Mrs Walker's ribbons. 'Mrs Walker, I want to tell you something.'

'Mother,' interposed Randolph, with his rough ends to his words, 'I tell you you've got to go. Eugenio'll raise something!'

'I'm not afraid of Eugenio,' said Daisy, with a toss of her head. 'Look here, Mrs Walker,' she went on, 'you know I'm coming to your party.'

'I am delighted to hear it.'

'I've got a lovely dress.'

'I am very sure of that.'

'But I want to ask a favour – permission to bring a friend.'

'I shall be happy to see any of your friends,' said Mrs Walker, turning with a smile to Mrs Miller.

'Oh, they are not my friends,' answered Daisy's mamma, smiling shyly, in her own fashion. 'I never spoke to them!'

'It's an intimate friend of mine – Mr Giovanelli,' said Daisy, without a tremor in her clear little voice, or a shadow on her brilliant little face.

Mrs Walker was silent a moment, she gave a rapid glance at Winterbourne. 'I shall be glad to see Mr Giovanelli,' she then said.

'He's an Italian,' Daisy pursued, with the prettiest serenity. 'He's a great friend of mine – he's the handsomest man in the world – except Mr Winterbourne! He knows plenty of Italians, but he wants to know some Americans. He thinks ever so much of Americans. He's tremendously clever. He's perfectly lovely!'

It was settled that this brilliant personage should be brought to Mrs Walker's party, and then Mrs Miller prepared to take her leave. 'I guess we'll go back to the hotel,' she said.

'You may go back to the hotel, mother, but I'm going to take a walk,' said Daisy.

'She's going to walk with Mr Giovanelli,' Randolph proclaimed.

'I am going to the Pincio,' said Daisy, smiling.

'Alone, my dear – at this hour?' Mrs Walker asked. The afternoon was drawing to a close – it was the hour for the throng of carriages and of contemplative pedestrians. 'I don't think it's safe, my dear,' said Mrs Walker.

'Neither do I,' subjoined Mrs Miller. 'You'll get the fever as sure as you live. Remember what Dr Davis told you!'

'Give her some medicine before she goes,' said Randolph.

The company had risen to its feet; Daisy, still showing her pretty teeth, bent over and kissed her hostess. 'Mrs Walker, you are too perfect,' she said. 'I'm not going alone; I am going to meet a friend.'

'Your friend won't keep you from getting the fever,' Mrs Miller observed.

'Is it Mr Giovanelli?' asked the hostess.

Winterbourne was watching the young girl; at this question his attention quickened. She stood there smiling and smoothing her bonnet-ribbons; she glanced at Winterbourne. Then, while she glanced and smiled, she answered without a shade of hesitation, 'Mr Giovanelli – the beautiful Giovanelli.'

'My dear young friend,' said Mrs Walker, taking her hand, pleadingly, 'don't walk off to the Pincio at this hour to meet a beautiful Italian.'

'Well, he speaks English,' said Mrs Miller.

'Gracious me!' Daisy exclaimed, 'I don't want to do anything improper. There's an easy way to settle it.' she continued to glance at Winterbourne. 'The Pincio is only a hundred yards distant; and if Mr Winterbourne were as polite as he pretends he would offer to walk with me!'

Winterbourne's politeness hastened to affirm itself, and the young girl gave him gracious leave to accompany her. They passed downstairs before her mother, and at the door Winterbourne perceived Mrs Miller's carriage drawn up, with the ornamental courier whose acquaintance he had made at Vevey seated within. 'Good-bye, Eugenio!' cried Daisy, 'I'm going to take a walk.' The distance from the Via Gregoriana to the beautiful garden at the other end of the Pincian Hill is, in fact, rapidly traversed. As the day was splendid, however, and the concourse of vehicles, walkers, and loungers numerous, the young Americans found their progress much delayed. This fact was highly agreeable to Winterbourne, in spite of his consciousness of his singular situation. The slow-moving, idly-gazing Roman crowd, bestowed much attention upon the extremely pretty young foreign lady who was passing through it upon his arm; and he wondered what on earth had been in Daisy's mind when she proposed to expose herself, unattended, to its appreciation. His own mission, to her sense apparently, was to consign her to the hands of Mr Giovanelli; but Winterbourne, at once annoyed and gratified, resolved that he would do no such thing.

'Why haven't you been to see me?' asked Daisy. 'You can't get out of that.'

'I have had the honour of telling you that I have only just stepped out of the train.'

'You must have stayed in the train a good while after it stopped!' cried the young girl, with her little laugh. 'I suppose you were asleep. You have had time to go to see Mrs Walker.'

'I knew Mrs Walker – ' Winterbourne began to explain.

'I knew where you knew her. You knew her at Geneva. She told me so. Well, you knew me at Vevey. That's just as good. So you ought to have come.' She asked him no other question than this; she began to prattle about her own affairs. 'We've got splendid rooms at the hotel; Eugenio says they're the best rooms in Rome. We are going to stay all winter – if we don't die of the fever; and I guess we'll stay then. It's a great deal nicer than I thought; I thought it would be fearfully quiet; I was sure it would be awfully poky. I was sure we should be going round all the time with one of those dreadful old men that explain about the pictures and things. But we only had about a week of that, and now I'm enjoying myself. I know ever so many people, and they are all so charming. The society's extremely select. There are all kinds – English, and Germans, and Italians. I think I like the English best. I like their style of conversation. But there are some lovely Americans. I never saw anything so hospitable. There's something or other every day. There's not much dancing; but I must say I never thought dancing was everything. I was always fond of conversation. I guess I shall have plenty at Mrs Walker's – her rooms are so small.' When they had passed the gate of the Pincian Gardens, Miss Miller began to wonder where Mr Giovanelli might be. 'We had better go straight to that place in front,' she said, 'where you look at the view.'

'I certainly shall not help you to find him,' Winterbourne declared.

'Then I shall find him without you,' said Miss Daisy.

'You certainly won't leave me!' cried Winterbourne.

She burst into her little laugh. 'Are you afraid you'll get lost – or run over? But there's Giovanelli, leaning against that tree. He's staring at the women in the carriages: did you ever see anything so cool?'

Winterbourne perceived at some distance a little man standing with folded arms, nursing his cane. He had a handsome face, an artfully-poised hat, a glass in one eye and a nosegay in his button-hole. Winterbourne looked at him a moment and then said, 'Do you mean to speak to that man?'

'Do I mean to speak to him? Why, you don't suppose I mean to communicate by signs?'

'Pray understand, then,' said Winterbourne, 'that I intend to remain with you.'

Daisy stopped and looked at him, without a sign of troubled consciousness in her face; with nothing but the presence of her charming eyes and her happy dimples. 'Well, she's a cool one!' thought the young man.

'I don't like the way you say that,' said Daisy. 'It's too imperious.'

'I beg your pardon if I say it wrong. The main point is to give you an idea of my meaning.'

The young girl looked at him more gravely, but with eyes that were prettier than ever. 'I have never allowed a gentleman to dictate to me, or to interfere with anything I do.'

'I think you have made a mistake,' said Winterbourne. 'You should sometimes listen to a gentleman – the right one!'

Daisy began to laugh again. 'I do nothing but listen to gentlemen!' she exclaimed. 'Tell me if Mr Giovanelli is the right one?'

The gentleman with the nosegay in his bosom had now perceived our two friends, and was approaching the young girl with obsequious rapidity. He bowed to Winterbourne as well as to the latter's companion; he had a brilliant smile, an intelligent eye; Winterbourne thought him not a bad-looking fellow. But he nevertheless said to Daisy – 'No, he's not the right one.'

Daisy evidently had a natural talent for performing introductions; she mentioned the name of each of her companions to the other. She strolled along with one of them on each side of her; Mr Giovanelli, who spoke English very cleverly – Winterbourne afterwards learned that he had practised the idiom upon a great many American heiresses – addressed her a great deal of very polite nonsense; he was extremely urbane, and the young American, who said nothing, reflected upon that profundity of Italian cleverness which enables people to appear more gracious in proportion as they are more acutely disappointed. Giovanelli, of course, had counted upon something more intimate; he had not bargained for a party of three. But he kept his temper in a manner which suggested far-stretching intentions. Winterbourne flattered himself that he had taken his measure. 'He is not a gentleman,' said the young American 'he is only a clever imitation of one. He is a music-master, or a penny-a-liner, or a third-rate artist. Damn his good looks!' Mr Giovanelli had certainly a very pretty face; but Winterbourne felt a superior indignation at his own lovely fellow-countrywoman's not knowing the difference between a spurious gentleman and a real one. Giovanelli chattered and jested and made himself wonderfully agreeable. It was time that if he was an imitation the imitation was very skilful. 'Nevertheless,' Winterbourne said to himself, 'a nice girl ought to know!' And then he came back to the question whether this was in fact a nice girl. Would a nice girl – even allowing for her being a little American flirt – make a rendezvous with a presumably low-lived foreigner? The rendezvous in this case, indeed, had been in broad daylight, and in the most crowded corner of Rome; but was it not impossible to regard the choice of these circumstances as a proof of extreme cynicism? Singular though it may seem, Winterbourne was vexed that the young girl, in joining her *amoroso*, should not appear more impatient of his own company, and he was vexed because of his inclination. It was impossible to regard her as a perfectly well-conducted young lady; she was wanting in a certain indispensable delicacy. It would therefore simplify matters greatly to be able to treat her as the object of one of those sentiments which are called by romancers 'lawless passions.' That she should seem to wish to get rid of him would help him to think more lightly of her, and to be able to think more lightly of her would make her much less perplexing. But

Daisy, on this occasion, continued to present herself as an inscrutable combination of audacity and innocence.

She had been walking some quarter of an hour, attended by her two cavaliers, and responding in a tone of very childish gaiety, as it seemed to Winterbourne, to the pretty speeches of Mr Giovanelli, when a carriage that had detached itself from the revolving train drew up beside the path. At the same moment Winterbourne perceived that his friend Mrs Walker – the lady whose house he had lately left – was seated in the vehicle and was beckoning to him. Leaving Miss Miller's side, he hastened to obey her summons. Mrs Walker was flushed; she wore an excited air. 'It is really too dreadful,' she said. 'That girl must not do this sort of thing. She must not walk here with you two men. Fifty people have noticed her.'

Winterbourne raised his eyebrows. 'I think it's a pity to make too much fuss about it.'

'It's a pity to let the girl ruin herself!'

'She is very innocent,' said Winterbourne.

'She is very crazy!' cried Mrs Walker. 'Did you ever see anything so imbecile as her mother? After you had all left me, just now, I could not sit still for thinking of it. It seemed too pitiful, not even to attempt to save her. I ordered the carriage and put on my bonnet, and came here as quickly as possible. Thank heaven I have found you!'

'What do you propose to do with us?' asked Winterbourne, smiling.

'To ask her to get in, to drive her about here for half an hour, so that the world may see she is not running absolutely wild, and then to take her safely home.'

'I don't think it's a very happy thought,' said Winterbourne; 'but you can try.'

Mrs Walker tried. The young man went in pursuit of Miss Miller, who had simply nodded and smiled at his interlocutrix in the carriage and had gone her way with her own companion. Daisy, on learning that Mrs Walker wished to speak to her, retraced her steps with a perfect good grace, and with Mr Giovanelli at her side. She declared that she was delighted to have a chance to present this gentleman to Mrs Walker. She immediately achieved the introduction, and declared that she had never in her life seen anything so lovely as Mrs Walker's carriage-rug.

'I am glad you admire it,' said this lady, smiling sweetly. 'Will you get in and let me put it over you?'

'Oh no, thank you,' said Daisy. 'I shall admire it much more as I see you driving round with it.'

'Do get in and drive with me,' said Mrs Walker.

'That would be charming, but it's so enchanting just as I am!' and Daisy gave a brilliant glance at the gentlemen on either side of her.

'It may be enchanting, dear child, but it is not the custom here,' urged Mrs Walker, leaning forward in her victoria with her hands devoutly clasped.

'Well it ought to be, then!' said Daisy. 'If I didn't walk I should expire.'

'You should walk with your mother, dear,' cried the lady from Geneva losing patience.

'With my mother dear!' exclaimed the young girl. Winterbourne saw that she scented interference. 'My mother never walked ten steps in her life. And then you know,' she added with a laugh, 'I am more than five years old.'

'You are old enough to be more reasonable. You are old enough, dear Miss Miller, to be talked about.'

Daisy looked at Mrs Walker, smiling intensely. 'Talked about? What do you mean?'

'Come into my carriage and I will tell you.'

Daisy turned her quickened glance again from one of the gentlemen beside her to the other. Mr Giovanelli was bowing to and fro, rubbing down his gloves and laughing very agreeably; Winterbourne thought it a most unpleasant scene. 'I don't think I want to know what you mean,' said Daisy presently. 'I don't think I should like it.'

Winterbourne wished that Mrs Walker would tuck in her carriage-rug and drive away; but this lady did not enjoy being defied, as she afterwards told him. 'Should you prefer being thought a very reckless girl?' she demanded

'Gracious me!' exclaimed Daisy. She looked again at Mr Giovanelli, then she turned to Winterbourne. There was a little pink flush in her cheek; she was tremendously pretty. 'Does Mr Winterbourne think,' she asked slowly, smiling, throwing back her head and glancing at him from head to foot, 'that – to save my reputation – I ought to get into the carriage?'

Winterbourne coloured; for an instant he hesitated greatly. It seemed so strange to hear her speak that way of her 'reputation.' But he himself, in fact, must speak in accordance with gallantry. The finest gallantry, here, was simply to tell her the truth; and the truth, for Winterbourne, as the few indications I have been able to give have made him known to the reader, was that Daisy Miller should take Mrs Walker's advice. He looked at her exquisite prettiness; and then he said very gently, 'I think you should get into the carriage.'

Daisy gave a violent laugh. 'I never heard anything so stiff! If this is improper, Mrs Walker,' she pursued, 'then I am all improper, and you must give me up. Good-bye; I hope you'll have a lovely ride!' and, with Mr Giovanelli, who made a triumphantly obsequious salute, she turned away.

Mrs Walker sat looking after her, and there were tears in Mrs Walker's eyes. 'Get in here, sir,' she said to Winterbourne, indicating the place beside her. The young man answered that he felt bound to accompany Miss Miller; whereupon Mrs Walker declared that if he refused her this favour she would never speak to him again. She was evidently in earnest. Winterbourne overtook Daisy and her companion, and offering the young girl his hand, told her that Mrs Walker had made an imperious claim upon his society. He expected that in answer she would say something rather free, something to commit herself still farther to that 'recklessness' from which Mrs Walker had so charitably endeavoured to dissuade her. But she only shook his hand, hardly looking at him, while Mr Giovanelli bade him farewell with a too emphatic flourish of the hat.

Winterbourne was not in the best possible humour as he took his seat in Mrs Walker's victoria. 'That was not clever of you,' he said candidly, while the vehicle mingled again with the throng of carriages.

'In such a case,' his companion answered, 'I don't wish to be clever, I wish to be *earnest!*'

'Well, your earnestness has only offended her and put her off.'

'It has happened very well,' said Mrs Walker. 'If she is so perfectly determined to compromise herself, the sooner one knows it the better; one can act accordingly.'

'I suspect she meant no harm,' Winterbourne rejoined.

'So I thought a month ago. But she has been going too far.'

'What has she been doing?'

'Everything that is not done here. Flirting with any man she could pick up, sitting in corners with mysterious Italians; dancing all the evening with the same partners; receiving visits at eleven o'clock at night. Her mother goes away when visitors come.'

'But her brother,' said Winterbourne, laughing, 'sits up till midnight.'

'He must be edified by what he sees. I'm told that at their hotel every one is talking about her, and that a smile goes round among the servants when a gentleman comes and asks for Miss Miller.'

'The servants be hanged!' said Winterbourne angrily. 'The poor girl's only fault,' he presently added, 'is that she is very uncultivated.'

'She is naturally indelicate,' Mrs Walker declared. 'Take that example this morning. How long had you known her at Vevey?'

'A couple of days.'

'Fancy, then, her making it a personal matter that you should have left the place!'

Winterbourne was silent for some moments, then he said, 'I suspect, Mrs Walker, that you and I have lived too long at Geneva!' And he added a request that she should inform him with what particular design she had made him enter her carriage.

'I wished to beg you to cease your relations with Miss Miller – not to flirt with her – to give her no farther opportunity to expose herself – to let her alone, in short.'

'I'm afraid I can't do that,' said Winterbourne. 'I like her extremely.'

'All the more reason that you shouldn't help her to make a scandal.'

'There shall be nothing scandalous in my attentions to her.'

'There certainly will be in the way she takes them. But I have said what I had on my conscience,' Mrs Walker pursued. 'If you wish to rejoin the young lady I will put you down. Here, by the way, you have a chance.'

The carriage was traversing that part of the Pincian Garden which overhangs the wall of Rome and overlooks the beautiful Villa Borghese. It is bordered by a large parapet, near which there are several seats. One of the seats, at a distance, was occupied by a gentleman and a lady, towards whom Mrs Walker gave a toss of her head. At the same moment these persons rose and walked towards the parapet. Winterbourne had asked the coachman to stop; he now descended from the carriage. His companion looked at him a moment in silence; then, while he raised his hat, she drove majestically away. Winterbourne stood there; he had turned his eyes towards Daisy and her cavalier. They evidently saw no one; they were too deeply occupied with each other. When they reached the low garden wall they stood a moment looking off at the great flat-topped pine clusters of the Villa Borghese; then Giovanelli seated himself familiarly upon the broad ledge of the wall. The western sun in the opposite sky sent out a brilliant shaft through a couple of cloud-bars, whereupon Daisy's companion took her parasol out of her hands and opened it. She came a little nearer, and he held the parasol over her; then, still holding it, he let it rest upon her shoulder, so that both of their heads were hidden from Winterbourne. This young man lingered a moment, then he began to walk. But he walked – not towards the couple with the parasol; towards the residence of his aunt, Mrs Costello.

Chapter 4

HE FLATTERED HIMSELF on the following day that there was no smiling among the servants when he, at least, asked for Mrs Miller at her hotel. This lady and her daughter, however, were not at home; and on the next day after, repeating his visit, Winterbourne again had the misfortune not to find them. Mrs Walker's party took place on the evening of the third day, and in spite of the frigidity of his last interview with the hostess Winterbourne was among the guests. Mrs Walker was one of those American ladies who, while residing abroad, make a point, in their own phrase, of studying European society; and she had on this occasion collected several specimens of her diversely-born fellow-mortals to serve, as it were, as text-books. When Winterbourne arrived Daisy Miller was not there; but in a few moments he saw her mother come in alone, very shyly and ruefully. Mrs Miller's hair, above her exposed-looking temples, was more frizzled than ever. As she approached Mrs Walker Winterbourne also drew near.

'You see I've come all alone,' said poor Mrs Miller. 'I'm so frightened; I don't know what to do; it's the first time I've ever been to a party alone – especially in this country. I wanted to bring Randolph or Eugenio, or some one, but Daisy just pushed me off by myself. I ain't used to going round alone.'

'And does not your daughter intend to favour us with her society?' demanded Mrs Walker, impressively.

'Well, Daisy's all dressed,' said Mrs Miller, with that accent of the dispassionate, if not of the philosophic, historian, with which she always recorded the current incidents of her daughter's career. 'She got dressed on purpose before dinner. But she's got a friend of hers there; that gentleman – the Italian – that she wanted to bring. They've got going at the piano; it seems as if they couldn't leave off. Mr Giovanelli sings splendidly. But I guess they'll come before very long,' concluded Mrs Miller hopefully.

'I'm sorry she should come – in that way,' said Mrs Walker.

'Well, I told her that there was no use in her getting dressed before dinner if she was going to wait three hours,' responded Daisy's mamma. 'I didn't see the use of her putting on such a dress as that to sit round with Mr Giovanelli.'

'This is most horrible!' said Mrs Walker, turning away and addressing herself to Winterbourne. '*Elle s'affiche.* It's her revenge for my having ventured to remonstrate with her. When she comes I shall not speak to her.'

Daisy came after eleven o'clock, but she was not, on such an occasion, a young lady to wait to be spoken to. She rustled forward in radiant loveliness, smiling and chattering, carrying a large bouquet, and attended by Mr Giovanelli. Every one stopped talking, and turned and looked at her. She came straight to Mrs Walker. 'I'm afraid you thought I never was coming, so I sent mother off to tell you. I wanted to make Mr Giovanelli practise some things before he came; you know he sings beautifully, and I want you to ask him to sing. This is Mr Giovanelli; you know I introduced him to you; he's got the most lovely voice, and he knows the most charming set of songs. I made him go over them this evening, on purpose; we had the greatest time at the hotel.' Of all this Daisy delivered herself with the sweetest, brightest audibleness looking now at her hostess and now round the room, while she gave a series of little pats, round her shoulders, to the edges of her dress. 'Is there any one I know?' she asked.

'I think every one knows you!' said Mrs Walker, pregnantly, and she gave a very cursory greeting to Mr Giovanelli. This gentleman bore himself gallantly. He smiled and bowed, and showed his white teeth, he curled his moustaches and rolled his eyes, and performed all the proper functions of a handsome Italian at an evening party. He sang, very prettily, half a dozen songs, though Mrs Walker afterwards declared that she had been quite unable to find out who asked him. It was apparently not Daisy who had given him his orders. Daisy sat at a distance from the piano, and though she had publicly, as it were, professed a high admiration for his singing, talked, not inaudibly, while it was going on.

'It's a pity these rooms are so small; we can't dance,' she said to Winterbourne, as if she had seen him five minutes before.

'I am not sorry we can't dance, 'Winterbourne answered; 'I don't dance.'

'Of course you don't dance; you're too stiff,' said Miss Daisy. 'I hope you enjoyed your drive with Mrs Walker.'

'No, I didn't enjoy it; I preferred walking with you.'

'We paired off, that was much better,' said Daisy. 'But did you ever hear anything so cool as Mrs Walker's wanting me to get into her carriage and drop poor Mr Giovanelli; and under the pretext that it was proper? People have different ideas! It would have been most unkind; he had been talking about that walk for ten days.'

'He should not have talked about it at all,' said Winterbourne; 'he would never have proposed to a young lady of this country to walk about the streets with him.'

'About the streets?' cried Daisy, with her pretty stare. 'Where, then, would he have proposed to her to walk? The Pincio is not the streets either; and I, thank goodness, am not a young lady of this country. The young ladies of this country have a dreadfully poky time of it, so far as I can learn; I don't see why I should change my habits for *them*.'

'I am afraid your habits are those of a flirt,' said Winterbourne, gravely.

'Of course they are,' she cried, giving him her little smiling stare again. 'I'm a fearful, frightful flirt! Did you ever hear of a nice girl that was not? But I suppose you will tell me now that I am not a nice girl.'

'You're a very nice girl, but I wish you would flirt with me, and me only,' said Winterbourne.

'Ah! thank you, thank you very much, you are the last man I should think of flirting with. As I have had the pleasure of informing you, you are too stiff.'

'You say that too often,' said Winterbourne.

Daisy gave a delighted laugh. 'If I could have the sweet hope of making you angry, I would say it again.'

'Don't do that; when I am angry I'm stiffer than ever. But if you won't flirt with me, do cease at least to flirt with your friend at the piano; they don't understand that sort of thing here.'

'I thought they understood nothing else!' exclaimed Daisy.

'Not in young unmarried women.'

'It seems to me much more proper in young unmarried women than in old married ones,' Daisy declared.

'Well,' said Winterbourne, 'when you deal with natives you must go by the custom of the place. Flirting is a purely American custom; it doesn't exist here. So when you show yourself in public with Mr Giovanelli, and without your mother – '

'Gracious! poor mother!' interposed Daisy.

'Though you may be flirting, Mr Giovanelli is not; he means something else.'

'He isn't preaching, at any rate,' said Daisy, with vivacity. 'And if you want very much to know, we are neither of us flirting; we are too good friends for that; we are very intimate friends.'

'Ah!' rejoined Winterbourne, 'if you are in love with each other it is another affair.'

She had allowed him up to this point to talk so frankly that he had no expectation of shocking her by this ejaculation; but she immediately got up, blushing visibly, and leaving him to exclaim mentally that little American flirts were the queerest creatures in the world. 'Mr Giovanelli, at least,' she said, giving her interlocutor a single glance, 'never says such very disagreeable things to me.'

Winterbourne was bewildered; he stood staring. Mr Giovanelli had finished singing; he left the piano and came over to Daisy. 'Won't you come into the other room and have some tea?' he asked, bending before her, with his decorative smile.

Daisy turned to Winterbourne, beginning to smile again. He was still more perplexed, for this inconsequent smile made nothing clear, though it seemed to prove, indeed, that she had a sweetness and softness that reverted instinctively to the pardon of offences. 'It has never occurred to Mr Winterbourne to offer me any tea,' she said, with her little tormenting manner.

'I have offered you advice,' Winterbourne rejoined.

'I prefer weak tea!' cried Daisy, and she went off with the brilliant Giovanelli. She sat with him in the adjoining room, in the embrasure of the window, for the rest of the evening. There was an interesting performance at the piano, but neither of these young people gave heed to it. When Daisy came to take leave of Mrs Walker, this lady conscientiously repaired the weakness of which she had been guilty at the moment of the young girl's arrival. She turned her back straight upon Miss Miller, and left her to depart with what grace she might. Winterbourne was standing near the door; he saw it all. Daisy turned very pale and looked at her mother, but Mrs Miller was humbly unconscious of any violation of the usual social forms. She appeared, indeed, to have felt an incongruous impulse to draw attention to her own striking observance of them. 'Good-night, Mrs Walker,' she said; 'we've had a beautiful evening. You see if I let Daisy come to parties without me, I don't want her to go away without me.' Daisy turned away, looking with a pale grave face at the circle near the door; Winterbourne saw that, for the first moment, she was too much shocked and puzzled even for indignation. He on his side was greatly touched.

'That was very cruel,' he said to Mrs Walker.

'She never enters my drawing-room again,' replied his hostess.

Since Winterbourne was not to meet her in Mrs Walker's drawing-room, he went as often as possible to Mrs Miller's hotel. The ladies were rarely at home, but when he found them the devoted Giovanelli was always present. Very often the polished little Roman was in the drawing-room with Daisy alone, Mrs Miller being apparently constantly of the opinion that discretion is the better part of surveillance. Winterbourne noted, at first with surprise, that Daisy on these occasions was never embarrassed or annoyed by his own entrance; but he very presently began to feel that she had no more surprises for him; the unexpected in her behaviour was the only thing to expect. She showed no displeasure at her *tête-à-tête* with Giovanelli being interrupted; she could chatter as freshly and freely with two gentlemen as with one; there was always in her conversation the same odd mixture of audacity and puerility. Winterbourne remarked to himself that, if she was seriously interested in Giovanelli, it was very singular that she should not take more trouble to preserve the sanctity of their interviews, and he liked her the more for her innocent-looking indifference and her apparently inexhaustible good-humour. He could hardly have said why, but she seemed to him a girl who would never be jealous. At the risk of exciting a somewhat derisive smile on the reader's part, I may affirm that, with regard to the women who had hitherto interested him, it very often seemed to Winterbourne among the possibilities that, given certain contingencies, he should be afraid – literally afraid – of these ladies. He had a pleasant sense that he should never be afraid of Daisy Miller. It must be added that this sentiment was not altogether flattering to Daisy; it was part of his conviction, or rather of his apprehension, that she would prove a very light young person.

But she was evidently very much interested in Giovanelli. She looked at him whenever he spoke; she was perpetually telling him to do this and to do that; she was constantly 'chaffing' and abusing him. She appeared completely to have forgotten that Winterbourne had said anything to displease her at Mrs Walker's little party. One Sunday afternoon, having gone to St Peter's with his aunt, Winterbourne perceived Daisy strolling about the great church in company with the inevitable Giovanelli. Presently he pointed out the young girl and her cavalier to Mrs Costello. This lady looked at them a moment through her eye-glass, and then she said:

'That's what makes you so pensive in these days, eh?'

'I had not the least idea I was pensive,' said the young man.

'You are very much preoccupied, you are thinking of something.'

'And what is it,' he asked, 'that you accuse me of thinking of?'

'Of that young lady's – Miss Baker's, Miss Chandler's – what's her name? – Miss Miller's intrigue with that little barber's block.'

'Do you call it an intrigue,' Winterbourne asked – 'an affair that goes on with such peculiar publicity?'

'That's their folly,' said Mrs Costello, 'it's not their merit.'

'No,' rejoined Winterbourne, with something of that pensiveness to which his aunt had alluded. 'I don't believe that there is anything to be called an intrigue.'

'I have heard a dozen people speak of it; they say she is quite carried away by him.'

'They are certainly very intimate,' said Winterbourne.

Mrs Costello inspected the young couple again with her optical instrument. 'He is very handsome. One easily sees how it is. She thinks him the most elegant man in the world, the finest gentleman. She has never seen anything like him; he is better even than the courier. It was the courier, probably, who introduced him, and if he succeeds in marrying the young lady, the courier will come in for a magnificent commission.'

'I don't believe she thinks of marrying him,' said Winterbourne, 'and I don't believe he hopes to marry her.'

'You may be very sure she thinks of nothing. She goes on from day to day, from hour to hour, as they did in the Golden Age. I can imagine nothing more vulgar. And at the same time,' added Mrs Costello, 'depend upon it that she may tell you any moment that she is "engaged." '

'I think that is more than Giovanelli expects,' said Winterbourne.

'Who is Giovanelli?'

'The little Italian. I have asked questions about him and learned something. He is apparently a perfectly respectable little man. I believe he is in a small way a *cavaliere avvocato*. But he doesn't move in what are called the first circles. I think it is really not absolutely impossible that the courier introduced him. He is evidently immensely charmed with Miss Miller. If she thinks him the finest gentleman in the world, he, on his side, has never found himself in personal contact with such splendour, such opulence, such expensiveness, as this young lady's. And then she must seem to him wonderfully pretty and interesting. I rather doubt whether he dreams of marrying her. That must appear to him too impossible a piece of luck. He has nothing but his handsome face to offer, and there is a substantial Mr Miller in that mysterious land of dollars. Giovanelli knows that he hasn't a title to offer. If he were only a count or a *marchese!* He must wonder at his luck at the way they have taken him up.'

'He accounts for it by his handsome face, and thinks Miss Miller a young lady *qui se passe ses fantaisies!*' said Mrs Costello.

'It is very true,' Winterbourne pursued, 'that Daisy and her mamma have not yet risen to that stage of – what shall I call it? – Of culture, at which the idea of catching a count or a *marchese* begins. I believe that they are intellectually incapable of that conception.'

'Ah! but the *cavaliere* can't believe it,' said Mrs Costello.

Of the observation excited by Daisy's 'intrigue,' Winterbourne gathered that day at St Peter's sufficient evidence. A dozen of the American colonists in Rome came to talk with Mrs Costello, who sat on a little portable stool at the base of one of the great pilasters. The vesper-service was going forward in splendid chants and organ-tones in the adjacent choir, and meanwhile, between Mrs Costello and her friends, there was a great deal said about poor little Miss Miller's going really 'too far.' Winterbourne was not pleased with what he heard; but when, coming out upon the great steps of the church, he saw Daisy, who had emerged before him, get into an open cab with her accomplice and roll away through the cynical streets of Rome, he could not deny to himself that she was going very far indeed. He felt very sorry for her – not exactly that he believed that she had completely lost her head, but because it was painful to hear so much that was pretty and undefended and natural assigned to a vulgar place among the categories of disorder. He made an attempt after this to give a hint to Mrs Miller. He met one day in the Corso a friend – a tourist like himself – who had just come out of the Doria Palace, where he had been walking through the beautiful gallery. His friend talked for a moment about the superb portrait of Innocent X. by Velasquez, which hangs in one of the cabinets of the palace, and then said, 'And in the same cabinet, by the way, I had the pleasure of contemplating a picture of a different kind – that pretty American girl whom you pointed out to me last week.' In answer to Winterbourne's inquiries, his friend narrated that the pretty American girl – prettier than ever – was seated with a companion in the secluded nook in which the great papal portrait is enshrined.

'Who was her companion?' asked Winterbourne.

'A little Italian with a bouquet in his button-hole. The girl is delightfully pretty, but I thought I under stood from you the other day that she was a young lady *du meilleur monde*.'

'So she is!' answered Winterbourne; and having assured himself that his informant had seen Daisy and her companion but five minutes before, he jumped into a cab and went to call on Mrs Miller. She was at home; but she apologised to him for receiving him in Daisy's absence.

'She's gone out somewhere with Mr Giovanelli,' said Mrs Miller. 'She's always going round with Mr Giovanelli.'

'I have noticed that they are very intimate,' Winterbourne observed.

'Oh! it seems as if they couldn't live without each other!' said Mrs

Miller. 'Well, he's a real gentleman, anyhow. I keep telling Daisy she's engaged!'

'And what does Daisy say?'

'Oh, she says she isn't engaged. But she might as well be!' this impartial parent resumed. 'She goes on as if she was. But I've made Mr Giovanelli promise to tell me, if *she* doesn't. I should want to write to Mr Miller about it – shouldn't you?'

Winterbourne replied that he certainly should; and the state of mind of Daisy's mamma struck him as so unprecedented in the annals of parental vigilance that he gave up as utterly irrelevant the attempt to place her upon her guard.

After this Daisy was never at home, and Winterbourne ceased to meet her at the houses of their common acquaintance, because, as he perceived, these shrewd people had quite made up their minds that she was going too far. They ceased to invite her, and they intimated that they desired to express to observant Europeans the great truth that, though Miss Daisy Miller was a young American lady, her behaviour was not representative – was regarded by her compatriots as abnormal. Winterbourne wondered how she felt about all the cold shoulders that were turned towards her, and sometimes it annoyed him to suspect that she did not feel at all. He said to himself that she was too light and childish, too uncultivated and unreasoning, too provincial, to have reflected upon her ostracism, or even to have perceived it. Then at other moments he believed that she carried about in her elegant and irresponsible little organism a defiant, passionate, perfectly observant consciousness of the impression she produced. He asked himself whether Daisy's defiance came from the consciousness of innocence or from her being, essentially, a young person of the reckless class. It must be admitted that holding oneself to a belief in Daisy's 'innocence' came to seem to Winterbourne more and more a matter of fine-spun gallantry. As I have already had occasion to relate, he was angry at finding himself reduced to chopping logic about this young lady; he was vexed at his want of instinctive certitude as to how far her eccentricities were generic, national, and how far they were personal. From either view of them he had somehow missed her, and now it was too late. She was 'carried away' by Mr Giovanelli.

A few days after his brief interview with her mother, he encountered her in that beautiful abode of flowering desolation known as the Palace of the Caesars. The early Roman spring had filled the air with bloom and perfume, and the rugged surface of the Palatine was muffled with tender verdure. Daisy was strolling along the top of one of those great mounds of ruin that are embanked with mossy marble and paved with monumental inscriptions. It seemed to him that Rome had never been so lovely as just then. He stood looking off at the enchanting harmony of line and colour that remotely encircles the city, inhaling the softly humid odours, and feeling the freshness of the year and the antiquity of the place reaffirm themselves in mysterious interfusion. It seemed to him also that Daisy had never looked so pretty; but this had been an observation of his whenever he met her. Giovanelli was at her side, and Giovanelli too wore an aspect of even unwonted brilliancy.

'Well,' said Daisy, 'I should think you would be lonesome!'

'Lonesome?' asked Winterbourne.

'You are always going round by yourself. Can't you get any one to walk with you?'

'I am not so fortunate,' said Winterbourne, 'as your companion.'

Giovanelli, from the first, had treated Winterbourne with distinguished politeness; he listened with a deferential air to his remarks; he laughed, punctiliously, at his pleasantries; he seemed disposed to testify to his belief that Winterbourne was a superior young man. He carried himself in no degree like a jealous wooer; he had obviously a great deal of tact; he had no objection to your expecting a little humility of him. It even seemed to Winterbourne at times that Giovanelli would find a certain mental relief in being able to have a private understanding with him – to say to him, as an intelligent man, that, bless you, *he* knew how extraordinary was this young lady, and didn't flatter himself with delusive – or at least *too* delusive – hopes of matrimony and dollars. On this occasion he strolled away from his companion to pluck a sprig of almond-blossom, which he carefully arranged in his button-hole.

'I know why you say that,' said Daisy, watching Giovanelli. 'Because you think I go round too much with *him!*' And she nodded at her attendant.

'Every one thinks so – if you care to know,' said Winterbourne.

'Of course I care to know!' Daisy exclaimed seriously. 'But I don't believe it. They are only pretending to be shocked. They don't really care a straw what I do. Besides, I don't go round so much.'

'I think you will find they do care. They will show it – disagreeably.'

Daisy looked at him a moment. 'How disagreeably?'

'Haven't you noticed anything?' Winterbourne asked.

'I have noticed you. But I noticed you were as stiff as an umbrella the first time I saw you.'

'You will find I am not so stiff as several others,' said Winterbourne, smiling.

'How shall I find it?'

'By going to see the others.'

'What will they do to me?'

'They will give you the cold shoulder. Do you know what that means?'

Daisy was looking at him intently; she began to colour. 'Do you mean as Mrs Walker did the other night?'

'Exactly!' said Winterbourne.

She looked away at Giovanelli, who was decorating himself with his almond-blossom. Then looking back at Winterbourne – 'I shouldn't think you would let people be so unkind!' she said.

'How can I help it?' he asked.

'I should think you would say something.'

'I do say something;' and he paused a moment. 'I say that your mother tells me that she believes you are engaged.'

'Well, she does,' said Daisy, very simply.

Winterbourne began to laugh. 'And does Randolph believe it?' he asked.

'I guess Randolph doesn't believe anything,' said Daisy. Randolph's scepticism excited Winterbourne to further hilarity, and he observed that Giovanelli was coming back to them. Daisy, observing it too, addressed herself again to her countryman. 'Since you have mentioned it,' she said, 'I am engaged.' . . . Winterbourne looked at her; he had stopped laughing. 'You don't believe it!' she added.

He was silent a moment; and then, 'Yes, I believe it!' he said.

'Oh no, you don't,' she answered 'Well, then – I am not!'

The young girl and her cicerone were on their way to the gate of the enclosure, so that Winterbourne, who had but lately entered, presently took leave of them. A week afterwards he went to dine at a beautiful villa on the Caelian Hill, and, on arriving, dismissed his hired vehicle. The evening was charming, and he promised himself the satisfaction of walking home beneath the Arch of Constantine and past the vaguely-lighted monuments of the Forum. There was a waning moon in the sky, and her radiance was not brilliant, but she was veiled in a thin cloud-curtain which seemed to diffuse and equalise it. When, on his return from the villa (it was eleven o'clock) Winterbourne approached the dusky circle of the Colosseum, it occurred to him, as a lover of the picturesque, that the interior, in the pale moonshine, would be well worth a glance. He turned aside and walked to one of the empty arches, near which, as he observed, an open carriage – one of the little Roman street cabs – was stationed. Then he passed in among the cavernous shadows of the great structure, and emerged upon the clear and silent arena. The place had never seemed to him more impressive. One-half of the gigantic circus was in deep shade; the other was sleeping in the luminous dusk. As he stood there he began to murmur Byron's famous lines, out of 'Manfred;' but before he had finished his quotation he remembered that if nocturnal meditations in the Colosseum are recommended by the poets, they are deprecated by the doctors. The historic atmosphere was there, certainly; but the historic atmosphere, scientifically considered, was no better than a villainous miasma. Winterbourne walked to the middle of the arena, to take a more general glance, intending thereafter to make a hasty retreat. The great cross in the centre was covered with shadow; it was only as he drew near it that he made it out distinctly. Then he saw that two persons were stationed upon the low steps which formed its base. One of these was a woman, seated; her companion was standing in front of her.

Presently the sound of the woman's voice came to him distinctly in the warm night air. 'Well, he looks at us as one of the old lions or tigers may have looked at the Christian martyrs!' These were the words he heard, in the familiar accent of Miss Daisy Miller.

'Let us hope he is not very hungry,' responded the ingenious Giovanelli. 'He will have to take me first; you will serve for dessert!'

Winterbourne stopped, with a sort of horror; and, it must be added, with a sort of relief. It was as if a sudden illumination had been flashed upon the ambiguity of Daisy's behaviour and the riddle had become easy to read. She was a young lady whom a gentleman need no longer be at pains to respect. He stood there looking at her – looking at her companion, and not reflecting that though he saw them vaguely, he himself must have been more brightly visible. He felt angry with himself that he had bothered so much about the right way of regarding Miss Daisy Miller. Then, as he was going to advance again, he checked himself; not from the fear that he was doing her injustice, but from a sense of the danger of appearing unbecomingly exhilarated by this sudden revulsion from cautious criticism. He turned away towards the entrance of the place; but as he did so he heard Daisy speak again.

'Why, it was Mr Winterbourne! He saw me – and he cuts me!'

What a clever little reprobate she was, and how smartly she played an injured innocence! But he wouldn't cut her. Winterbourne came forward again, and went towards the great cross. Daisy had got up; Giovanelli lifted his hat. Winterbourne had now begun to think simply of the craziness, from a sanitary point of view, of a delicate young girl lounging away the evening in this nest of malaria. What if she *were* a clever little reprobate? that was no reason for her dying of the *pernicosa*. 'How long have you been here?' he asked, almost brutally.

Daisy, lovely in the flattering moonlight, looked at him a moment. Then – 'All the evening,' she answered gently ... 'I never saw anything so pretty.'

'I am afraid,' said Winterbourne, 'that you will not think Roman fever very pretty. This is the way people catch it. I wonder,' he added, turning to Giovanelli, 'that you, a native Roman, should countenance such a terrible indiscretion.'

'Ah,' said the handsome native, 'for myself, I am not afraid.'

'Neither am I – for you! I am speaking for this young lady.'

Giovanelli lifted his well-shaped eyebrows and showed his brilliant teeth. But he took Winterbourne's rebuke with docility. 'I told the Signorina it was a grave indiscretion; but when was the Signorina ever prudent?'

'I never was sick, and I don't mean to be!' the Signorina declared. 'I don't look like much, but I'm healthy! I was bound to see the Colosseum by moonlight; I shouldn't have wanted to go home without that; and we have had the most beautiful time, haven't we, Mr Giovanelli? If there has been any danger, Eugenio can give me some pills. He has got some splendid pills.'

'I should advise you,' said Winterbourne, 'to drive home as fast as possible and take one!'

'What you say is very wise,' Giovanelli rejoined. 'I will go and make sure the carriage is at hand.' And he went forward rapidly.

Daisy followed with Winterbourne. He kept looking at her, she seemed not in the least embarrassed. Winterbourne said nothing; Daisy chattered about the beauty of the place. 'Well, *I have* seen the Colosseum by moonlight!' she exclaimed. 'That's one good thing.'

Then, noticing Winterbourne's silence, she asked him why he didn't speak. He made no answer; he only began to laugh. They passed under one of the dark archways; Giovanelli was in front with the carriage. Here Daisy stopped a moment, looking at the young American. '*Did* you believe I was engaged the other day?' she asked.

'It doesn't matter what I believed the other day,' said Winterbourne, still laughing.

'Well, what do you believe now?'

'I believe that it makes very little difference whether you are engaged or not!'

He felt the young girl's pretty eyes fixed upon him through the thick gloom of the archway; she was apparently going to answer. But

Giovanelli hurried her forward. 'Quick, quick,' he said; 'if we get in by midnight we are quite safe.'

Daisy took her seat in the carriage, and the fortunate Italian placed himself beside her. 'Don't forget Eugenio's pills!' said Winterbourne, as he lifted his hat.

'I don't care,' said Daisy, in a little strange tone, 'whether I have Roman fever or not!' Upon this the cab driver cracked his whip, and they rolled away over the desultory patches of the antique pavement.

Winterbourne – to do him justice, as it were – mentioned to no one that he had encountered Miss Miller, at midnight, in the Colosseum with a gentleman; but nevertheless, a couple of days later, the fact of her having been there under these circumstances was known to every member of the little American circle, and commented accordingly. Winterbourne reflected that they had of course known it at the hotel, and that, after Daisy's return, there had been an exchange of jokes between the porter and the cab-driver But the young man was conscious, at the same moment, that it had ceased to be a matter of serious regret to him that the little American flirt should be 'talked about' by low-minded menials. These people, a day or two later, had serious information to give: the little American flirt was alarmingly ill. Winterbourne, when the rumour came to him, immediately went to the hotel for more news. He found that two or three charitable friends had preceded him, and that they were being entertained in Mrs Miller's salon by Randolph.

'It's going round at night,' said Randolph – 'that's what made her sick. She's always going round at night. I shouldn't think she'd want to – it's so plaguey dark. You can't see anything here at night, except when there's a moon. In America there's always a moon!' Mrs Miller was invisible: she was now, at least, giving her daughter the advantage of her society. It was evident that Daisy was dangerously ill.

Winterbourne went often to ask for news of her, and once he saw Mrs Miller who, though deeply alarmed, was – rather to his surprise – perfectly composed, and, as it appeared, a most efficient and judicious nurse. She talked a good deal about Dr Davis, but Winterbourne paid her the compliment of saying to himself that she was not, after all, such a monstrous goose. 'Daisy spoke of you the other day,' she said to him. 'Half the time she doesn't know what she's saying, but that time I think she did. She gave me a message; she told me to tell you. She told me to tell you that she never was engaged to that handsome Italian. I am sure I am very glad; Mr Giovanelli hasn't been near us since she was taken ill. I thought he was so much of a gentleman; but I don't call that very polite! A lady told me that he was afraid I was angry with him for taking Daisy round at night. Well, so I am; but I suppose he knows I'm a lady. I would scorn to scold him. Any way, she says she's not engaged. I don't know why she wanted you to know; but she said to me three times – "Mind you tell Mr Winterbourne." And then she told me to ask if you remembered the time you went to that castle, in Switzerland. But I said I wouldn't give any such messages as that. Only, if she is not engaged, I'm sure I'm glad to know it.'

But, as Winterbourne had said, it mattered very little. A week after this the poor girl died; it had been a terrible case of the fever. Daisy's grave was in the little Protestant cemetery, in an angle of the wall of imperial Rome, beneath the cypresses and the thick spring flowers. Winterbourne stood there beside it, with a number of other mourners; a number larger than the scandal excited by the young lady's career would have led you to expect. Near him stood Giovanelli, who came nearer still before Winterbourne turned away. Giovanelli was very pale; on this occasion he had no flower in his button hole, he seemed to wish to say something. At last he said, 'She was the most beautiful young lady I ever saw, and the most amiable.' And then he added in a moment, 'And she was the most innocent.'

Winterbourne looked at him, and presently repeated his words, 'And the most innocent?'

'The most innocent!'

Winterbourne felt sore and angry. 'Why the devil, 'he asked, 'did you take her to that fatal place?'

Mr Giovanelli's urbanity was apparently imperturbable. He looked on the ground a moment, and then he said, 'For myself, I had no fear; and she wanted to go.'

'That was no reason!' Winterbourne declared.

The subtle Roman again dropped his eyes. 'If she had lived, I should have got nothing. She would never have married me, I am sure.'

'She would never have married you?'

'For a moment I hoped so. But no. I am sure.'

Winterbourne listened to him; he stood staring at the raw protuberance among the April daisies. When he turned away again Mr Giovanelli, with his light slow step, had retired.

Winterbourne almost immediately left Rome; but the following summer he again met his aunt, Mrs Costello, at Vevey. Mrs Costello was fond of Vevey. In the interval Winterbourne had often thought of Daisy Miller and her mystifying manners. One day he spoke of her to his aunt – said it was on his conscience that he had done her injustice.

'I am sure I don't know,' said Mrs Costello. 'How did your injustice affect her?'

'She sent me a message before her death which I didn't understand at the time. But I have understood it since. She would have appreciated one's esteem.'

'Is that a modest way,' asked Mrs Costello, 'of saying that she would have reciprocated one's affection?"

Winterbourne offered no answer to this question; but he presently said, 'You were right in that remark that you made last summer. I was booked to make a mistake. I have lived too long in foreign parts.'

Nevertheless, he went back to live at Geneva, whence there continue to come the most contradictory accounts of his motives of sojourn: a report that he is 'studying' hard – an intimation that he is much interested in a very clever foreign lady.

FOUR MEETINGS

I saw her only four times, but I remember them vividly; she made an impression upon me. I thought her very pretty and very interesting – a charming specimen of a type. I am very sorry to hear of her death; and yet, when I think of it, why should I be sorry? The last time I saw her she was certainly not –   But I will describe all our meetings in order.

Chapter 1

The first one took place in the country, at a little tea-party, one snowy night. It must have been some seventeen years ago. My friend Latouche, going to spend Christmas with his mother, had persuaded me to go with him, and the good lady had given in our honour the entertainment of which I speak. To me it was really entertaining; I had never been in the depths of New England at that season. It had been snowing all day, and the drifts were knee-high. I wondered how the ladies had made their way to the house; but I perceived that at Grimwinter a conversazione offering the attraction of two gentlemen from New York was felt to be worth an effort.

Mrs Latouche, in the course of the evening, asked me if I 'didn't want to' show the photographs to some of the young ladies. The photographs were in a couple of great portfolios, and had been brought home by her son, who, like myself, was lately returned from Europe. I looked round and was struck with the fact that most of the young ladies were provided with an object of interest more absorbing than the most vivid sun-picture. But there was a person standing alone near the mantelshelf, and looking round the room with a small gentle smile which seemed at odds, somehow, with her isolation. I looked at her a moment, and then said, 'I should like to show them to that young lady.'

'Oh yes,' said Mrs Latouche, 'she is just the person. She doesn't care for flirting; I will speak to her.'

I rejoined that if she did not care for flirting, she was, perhaps, not just the person; but Mrs Latouche had already gone to propose the photographs to her.

'She's delighted,' she said, coming back. 'She is just the person, so quiet and so bright. 'And then she told me the young lady was, by name, Miss Caroline Spencer, and with this she introduced me.

Miss Caroline Spencer was not exactly a beauty, but she was a charming little figure. She must have been close upon thirty, but she was made almost like a little girl, and she had the complexion of a child. She had a very pretty head, and her hair was arranged as nearly as possible like the hair of a Greek bust, though indeed it was to be doubted if she had ever seen a Greek bust. She was 'artistic,' I suspected, so far as Grimwinter allowed such tendencies. She had a soft, surprised eye, and thin lips, with very pretty teeth. Round her neck she wore what ladies call, I believe, a 'ruche,' fastened with a very small pin in pink coral, and in her hand she carried a fan made of plaited straw and adorned with pink ribbon. She wore a scanty black silk dress. She spoke with a kind of soft precision, showing her white teeth between her narrow but tender-looking lips, and she seemed extremely pleased, even a little fluttered, at the prospect of my demonstrations. These went forward very smoothly, after I had moved the portfolios out of their corner and placed a couple of chairs near a lamp. The photographs were usually things I knew – large views of Switzerland, Italy, and Spain, landscapes, copies of famous buildings, pictures, and statues. I said what I could about them, and my companion, looking at them as I held them up, sat perfectly still, with her straw fan raised to her under-lip. Occasionally, as I laid one of the pictures down, she said very softly, 'Have you seen that place?' I usually answered that I had seen it several times (I had been a great traveller), and then I felt that she looked at me askance for a moment with her pretty eyes. I had asked her at the outset whether she had been to Europe; to this she answered, 'No, no, no,' in a little quick, confidential whisper. But after that, though she never took her eyes off the pictures, she said so little that I was afraid she was bored. Accordingly, after we had finished one portfolio, I offered, if she desired it, to desist. I felt that she was not bored, but her reticence puzzled me, and I wished to make her speak. I turned round to look at her, and saw that there was a faint flush in each of her cheeks. She was waving her little fan to and fro. Instead of looking at me she fixed her eyes upon the other portfolio, which was leaning against the table.

'Won't you show me that?' she asked, with a little tremor in her voice. I could almost have believed she was agitated.

'With pleasure,' I answered, 'if you are not tired.'

'No, I am not tired,' she affirmed. 'I like it – I love it.'

And as I took up the other portfolio she laid her hand upon it, rubbing it softly.

'And have you been here too?' she asked.

On my opening the portfolio it appeared that I had been there. One of the first photographs was a large view of the Castle of Chillon, on the Lake of Geneva.

'Here,' I said, 'I have been many a time. Is it not beautiful?' And I pointed to the perfect reflection of the rugged rocks and pointed towers in the clear still water. She did not say, 'Oh, enchanting!' and push it away to see the next picture. She looked a while and then she asked if it was not where Bonivard, about whom Byron wrote, was confined. I assented, and tried to quote some of Byron's verses, but in this attempt I succeeded imperfectly.

She fanned herself a moment, and then repeated the lines correctly, in a soft, flat, and yet agreeable voice. By the time she had finished she was blushing. I complimented her and told her she was perfectly equipped for visiting Switzerland and Italy. She looked at me askance again, to see whether I was serious, and I added, that if she wished to recognise Byron's descriptions she must go abroad speedily; Europe was getting sadly dis-Byronised.

'How soon must I go?' she asked.

'Oh, I will give you ten years.'

'I think I can go within ten years,' she answered very soberly.

'Well,' I said, 'you will enjoy it immensely; you will find it very charming.' And just then I came upon a photograph of some nook in a foreign city which I had been very fond of, and which recalled tender memories. I discoursed (as I suppose) with a certain eloquence; my companion sat listening, breathless.

'Have you been *very* long in foreign lands?' she asked, some time after I had ceased.

'Many years,' I said.

'And have you travelled everywhere?'

'I have travelled a great deal. I am very fond of it; and, happily, I have been able.'

Again she gave me her sidelong gaze. 'And do you know the foreign languages?'

'After a fashion.'

'Is it hard to speak them?'

'I don't believe you would find it hard,' I gallantly responded.

'Oh, I shouldn't want to speak – I should only want to listen,' she said. Then, after a pause, she added – 'They say the French theatre is so beautiful.'

'It is the best in the world.'

'Did you go there very often?'

'When I was first in Paris I went every night.'

'Every night!' And she opened her clear eyes very wide. 'That to me is – ' and she hesitated a moment – 'is very wonderful.' A few minutes later she asked – 'Which country do you prefer?'

'There is one country I prefer to all others. I think you would do the same.'

She looked at me a moment, and then she said softly – 'Italy?'

'Italy,' I answered softly, too; and for a moment we looked at each other. She looked as pretty as if, instead of showing her photographs, I had been making love to her. To increase the analogy, she glanced away, blushing. There was a silence, which she broke at last by saying –

'That is the place which – in particular – I thought of going to.'

'Oh, that's the place – that's the place!' I said.

She looked at two or three photographs in silence. 'They say it is not so dear.'

'As some other countries? Yes, that is not the least of its charms.'

'But it is all very dear, is it not?'

'Europe, you mean?'

'Going there and travelling. That has been the trouble. I have very little money. I give lessons,' said Miss Spencer.

'Of course one must have money,' I said, 'but one can manage with a moderate amount.'

'I think I should manage. I have laid something by, and I am always adding a little to it. It's all for that.' She paused a moment, and then went on with a kind of suppressed eagerness, as if telling me the story were a rare, but a possibly impure satisfaction. 'But it has not been only the money; it has been everything. Everything has been against it. I have waited and waited. It has been a mere castle in the air. I am almost afraid to talk about it. Two or three times it has been a little nearer, and then I have talked about it and it has melted away. I have talked about it too much,' she said, hypocritically; for I saw that such talking was now a small tremulous ecstasy. 'There is a lady who is a great friend of mine; she doesn't want to go; I always talk to her about it. I tire her dreadfully. She told me once she didn't know what would become of me. I should go crazy if I did not go to Europe, and I should certainly go crazy if I did.'

'Well,' I said, 'you have not gone yet, and nevertheless you are not crazy.'

She looked at me a moment, and said – 'I am not so sure. I don't think of anything else. I am always thinking of it. It prevents me from thinking of things that are nearer home – things that I ought to attend to. That is a kind of craziness.'

'The cure for it is to go,' I said.

'I have a faith that I shall go. I have a cousin in Europe!' she announced.

We turned over some more photographs, and I asked her if she had always lived at Grimwinter.

'Oh no, sir,' said Miss Spencer. 'I have spent twenty-three months in Boston.'

I answered, jocosely, that in that case foreign lands would probably prove a disappointment to her; but I quite failed to alarm her.

'I know more about them than you might think,' she said, with her shy, neat little smile. 'I mean by reading; I have read a great deal. I have not only read Byron; I have read histories and guide-books. I know I shall like it!'

'I understand your case,' I rejoined. 'You have the native American passion – the passion for the picturesque. With us, I think it is primordial – antecedent to experience. Experience comes and only shows us something we have dreamt of.'

'I think that is very true,' said Caroline Spencer. 'I have dreamt of everything; I shall know it all!'

'I am afraid you have wasted a great deal of time.'

'Oh yes, that has been my great wickedness.'

The people about us had begun to scatter; they were taking their leave. She got up and put out her hand to me, timidly, but with a peculiar brightness in her eyes.

'I am going back there,' I said, as I shook hands with her. 'I shall look out for you.'

'I will tell you,' she answered, 'if I am disappointed.'

And she went away, looking delicately agitated, and moving her little straw fan.

Chapter 2

A FEW MONTHS AFTER THIS I returned to Europe, and some three years elapsed. I had been living in Paris, and, toward the end of October, I went from that city to Havre, to meet my sister and her husband, who had written me that they were about to arrive there. On reaching Havre I found that the steamer was already in; I was nearly two hours late. I repaired directly to the hotel, where my relatives were already established. My sister had gone to bed, exhausted and disabled by her voyage; she was a sadly incompetent sailor, and her sufferings on this occasion had been extreme. She wished, for the moment, for undisturbed rest, and was unable to see me more than five minutes; so it was agreed that we should remain at Havre until the next day. My brother-in-law, who was anxious about his wife, was unwilling to leave her room; but she insisted upon his going out with me to take a walk and recover his land-legs. The early autumn day was warm and charming, and our stroll through the bright-coloured, busy streets of the old French seaport was sufficiently entertaining We walked along the sunny, noisy quays, and then turned into a wide, pleasant street, which lay half in sun and half in shade – a French provincial street, that looked like an old water-colour drawing: tall, gray, steep-roofed, red-gabled, many-storied houses; green shutters on windows and old scroll-work above them; flower-pots in balconies, and white-capped women in doorways. We walked in the shade; all this stretched away on the sunny side of the street and made a picture. We looked at it as we passed along; then, suddenly, my brother-in-law stopped – pressing my arm and staring. I followed his gaze and saw that we had paused just before coming to a café, where, under an awning, several tables and chairs were disposed upon the pavement. The windows were open behind; half a dozen plants in tubs were ranged beside the door; the pavement was besprinkled with clean bran. It was a nice little, quiet, old-fashioned café; inside, in the comparative dusk, I saw a stout handsome woman, with pink ribbons in her cap, perched up with a mirror behind her back, smiling at some one who was out of sight. All this, however, I perceived afterwards; what I first observed was a lady sitting alone, outside, at one of the little marble-topped tables. My brother-in-law had stopped to look at her. There was something on the little table, but she was leaning back quietly, with her hands folded, looking down the street, away from us. I saw her only in some thing less than profile; nevertheless, I instantly felt that had seen her before.

'The little lady of the steamer!' exclaimed my brother-in-law.

'Was she on your steamer?' I asked.

'From morning till night. She was never sick. She used to sit perpetually at the side of the vessel with her hands crossed that way, looking at the eastward horizon.'

'Are you going to speak to her?'

'I don't know her. I never made acquaintance with her. I was too seedy. But I used to watch her and – I don't know why – to be interested in her. She's a dear little Yankee woman. I have an idea she is a schoolmistress taking a holiday – for which her scholars have made up a purse.'

She turned her face a little more into profile, looking at the steep gray house fronts opposite to her. Then I said – 'I shall speak to her myself.'

'I wouldn't; she is very shy,' said my brother-in-law.

'My dear fellow, I know her. I once showed her photographs at a tea-party.'

And I went up to her. She turned and looked at me, and I saw she was in fact Miss Caroline Spencer. But she was not so quick to recognise me; she looked startled. I pushed a chair to the table and sat down.

'Well,' I said, 'I hope you are not disappointed!'

She stared, blushing a little; then she gave a small jump which betrayed recognition.

'It was you who showed me the photographs – at Grimwinter!'

'Yes, it was I. This happens very charmingly, for I feel as if it were for me to give you a formal reception here – an official welcome. I talked to you so much about Europe.'

'You didn't say too much. I am so happy!' she softly exclaimed.

Very happy she looked. There was no sign of her being older; she was as gravely, decently, demurely pretty as before. If she had seemed before a thin-stemmed, mild-hued flower of Puritanism, it may be imagined whether in her present situation this delicate bloom was less apparent. Beside her an old gentleman was drinking absinthe; behind her the *dame de comptoir* in the pink ribbons was calling 'Alcibiade! Alcibiade!' to the long-aproned waiter. I explained to Miss Spencer that my companion had lately been her shipmate, and my brother-in-law came up and was introduced to her. But she looked at him as if she had never seen him before, and I remembered that he had told me that her eyes were always fixed upon the eastward horizon. She had evidently not noticed him, and, still timidly smiling, she made no attempt whatever to pretend that she had. I stayed with her at the café door, and he went back to the hotel and to his wife. I said to Miss Spencer that this meeting of ours in the first hour of her landing was really very strange, but that I was delighted to be there and receive her first impressions.

'Oh, I can't tell you,' she said; 'I feel as if I were in a dream. I have been sitting here for an hour, and I don't want to move. Everything is so picturesque. I don't know whether the coffee has intoxicated me; it's so delicious.'

'Really,' said I, 'if you are so pleased with this poor prosaic Havre, you will have no admiration left for better things. Don't spend your admiration all the first day; remember it's your intellectual letter of credit. Remember all the beautiful places and things that are waiting for you; remember that lovely Italy!'

'I'm not afraid of running short,' she said gaily, still looking at the opposite houses. 'I could sit here all day, saying to myself that here I am at last. It's so dark, and old, and different.'

'By the way,' I inquired, 'how come you to be sitting here? Have you not gone to one of the inns?' For I was half amused, half alarmed, at the good conscience with which this delicately pretty woman had stationed herself in conspicuous isolation on the edge of the sidewalk.

'My cousin brought me here,' she answered. 'You know I told you I had a cousin in Europe. He met me at the steamer this morning.'

'It was hardly worth his while to meet you if he was to desert you so soon'

'Oh, he has only left me for half an hour,' said Miss Spencer. 'He has gone to get my money.'

'Where is your money?'

She gave a little laugh. 'It makes me feel very fine to tell you! It is in some circular notes.'

'And where are your circular notes?'

'In my cousin's pocket.'

This statement was very serenely uttered, but – I can hardly say why – it gave me a sensible chill. At the moment I should have been utterly unable to give the reason of this sensation, for I knew nothing of Miss Spencer's cousin. Since he was her cousin, the presumption was in his favour. But I felt suddenly uncomfortable at the thought that, half an hour after her landing, her scanty funds should have passed into his hands.

'Is he to travel with you?' I asked.

'Only as far as Paris. He is an art-student in Paris. I wrote to him that I was coming, but I never expected him to come off to the ship. I supposed he would only just meet me at the train in Paris. It is very kind of him. But he *is* very kind – and very bright.'

I instantly became conscious of an extreme curiosity to see this bright cousin who was an art-student

'He is gone to the banker's?' I asked.

'Yes, to the banker's. He took me to an hotel – such a queer, quaint, delicious little place, with a court in the middle, and a gallery all round, and a lovely landlady, in such a beautifully-fluted cap, and such a perfectly-fitting dress! After a while we came out to walk to the banker's, for I haven't got any French money.

But I was very dizzy from the motion of the vessel, and I thought I had better sit down. He found this place for me here, and he went off to the banker's himself. I am to wait here till he comes back.'

It may seem very fantastic, but it passed through my mind that he would never come back. I settled myself in my chair beside Miss Spencer and determined to await the event. She was extremely observant; there was something touching in it. She noticed everything that the movement of the street brought before us – peculiarities of costume, the shapes of vehicles, the big Norman horses, the fat priests, the shaven poodles. We talked of these things, and there was something charming in her freshness of perception and the way her book-nourished fancy recognised and welcomed everything.

'And when your cousin comes back, what are you going to do?' I asked.

She hesitated a moment. 'We don't quite know.'

'When do you go to Paris? If you go by the four o'clock train, I may have the pleasure of making the journey with you.'

'I don't think we shall do that. My cousin thinks I had better stay here a few days.'

'Oh!' said I; and for five minutes said nothing more. I was wondering what her cousin was, in vulgar parlance, 'up to.' I looked up and down the street, but saw nothing that looked like a bright American art-student. At last I took the liberty of observing that Havre was hardly a place to choose as one of the aesthetic stations of a European tour. It was a place of convenience, nothing more; a place of transit, through which transit should be rapid. I recommended her to go to Paris by the afternoon train, and meanwhile to amuse herself by driving to the ancient fortress at the mouth of the harbour – that picturesque circular structure which bore the name of Francis the First, and looked like a small castle of St Angelo. (It has lately been demolished.)

She listened with much interest; then for a moment she looked grave.

'My cousin told me that when he returned he should have something particular to say to me, and that we could do nothing or decide nothing until I should have heard it. But I will make him tell me quickly, and then we will go to the ancient fortress. There is no hurry to get to Paris; there is plenty of time.'

She smiled with her softly severe little lips as she spoke those last words. But I, looking at her with a purpose, saw just a tiny gleam of apprehension in her eye.

'Don't tell me,' I said, 'that this wretched man is going to give you bad news!'

'I suspect it is a little bad, but I don't believe it is very bad. At any rate, I must listen to it.'

I looked at her again an instant. 'You didn't come to Europe to listen,' I said. 'You came to see!' But now I was sure her cousin would come back; since he had something disagreeable to say to her, he certainly would turn up. We sat a while longer, and I asked her about her plans of travel. She had them on her fingers' ends, and she told over the names with a kind of solemn distinctness; from Paris to Dijon and to Avignon, from Avignon to Marseilles and the Cornice road; thence to Genoa, to Spezia, to Pisa, to Florence, to Rome. It apparently had never occurred to her that there could be the least incommodity in her travelling alone; and since she was unprovided with a companion I of course scrupulously abstained from disturbing her sense of security.

At last her cousin came back. I saw him turn towards us out of a side street, and from the moment my eyes rested upon him I felt that this was the bright American art-student. He wore a slouch hat and a rusty black velvet jacket, such as I had often encountered in the Rue Bonaparte. His shirt-collar revealed a large section of a throat which, at a distance, was not strikingly statuesque. He was tall and lean; he had red hair and freckles. So much I had time to observe while he approached the café, staring at me with natural surprise from under his umbrageous coiffure. When he came up to us I immediately introduced myself to him as an old acquaintance of Miss Spencer. He looked at me hard with a pair of little red eyes, then he made me a solemn bow in the French fashion, with his sombrero.

'You were not on the ship?' he said.

'No, I was not on the ship. I have been in Europe these three years.'

He bowed once more, solemnly, and motioned me to be seated again. I sat down, but it was only for the purpose of observing him an instant – I saw it was time I should return to my sister. Miss Spencer's cousin was a queer fellow. Nature had not shaped him for a Raphaelesque or Byronic attire, and his velvet doublet and naked throat were not in harmony with his facial attributes. His hair was cropped close to his head; his ears were large and ill-adjusted to the same. He had a lackadaisical carriage and a sentimental droop which were peculiarly at variance with his keen strange-coloured eyes. Perhaps I was prejudiced, but I thought his eyes treacherous. He said nothing for some time; he leaned his hands on his cane and looked up and down the street. Then at last, slowly lifting his cane and pointing with it, 'That's a very nice bit,' he remarked, softly. He had his head on one side, and his little eyes were half closed. I followed the direction of his stick; the object it indicated was a red cloth hung out of an old window. 'Nice bit of colour,' he continued; and without moving his head he transferred his half-closed gaze to me. 'Composes well,' he pursued. 'Make a nice thing.' He spoke in a hard vulgar voice.

'I see you have a great deal of eye,' I replied. 'Your cousin tells me you are studying art.' He looked at me in the same way without answering, and I went on with deliberate urbanity – 'I suppose you are at the studio of one of those great men.'

Still he looked at me, and then he said softly – 'Gérome.'

'Do you like it?' I asked.

'Do you understand French?' he said.

'Some kinds,' I answered.

He kept his little eyes on me; then he said – 'J'adore la peinture!'

'Oh, I understand that kind!' I rejoined. Miss Spencer laid her hand upon her cousin's arm with a little pleased and fluttered movement; it was delightful to be among people who were on such easy terms with foreign tongues. I got up to take leave, and asked Miss Spencer where, in Paris, I might have the honour of waiting upon her. To what hotel would she go?

She turned to her cousin inquiringly, and he honoured me again with his little languid leer. 'Do you know the Hotel des Princes?'

'I know where it is.'

'I shall take her there.'

'I congratulate you,' I said to Caroline Spencer. 'I believe it is the best inn in the world; and in case I should still have a moment to call upon you here, where are you lodged?'

'Oh, it's such a pretty name,' said Miss Spencer, gleefully. 'À la Belle Normande.'

As I left them her cousin gave me a great flourish with his picturesque hat.

Chapter 3

MY SISTER, AS IT PROVED, was not sufficiently restored to leave Havre by the afternoon train; so that, as the autumn dusk began to fall, I found myself at liberty to call at the sign of the Fair Norman. I must confess that I had spent much of the interval in wondering what the disagreeable thing was that my charming friend's disagreeable cousin had been telling her. The 'Belle Normande' was a modest inn in a shady by-street, where it gave me satisfaction to think Miss Spencer must have encountered local colour in abundance. There was a crooked little court, where much of the hospitality of the house was carried on; there was a staircase climbing to bedrooms on the outer side of the wall; there was a small trickling fountain with a stucco statuette in the midst of it; there was a little boy in a white cap and apron cleaning copper vessels at a conspicuous kitchen door; there was a chattering landlady, neatly laced, arranging apricots and grapes into an artistic pyramid upon a pink plate. I looked about, and on a green bench outside of an open door labelled *Salle à Manger*, I perceived Caroline Spencer. No sooner had I looked at her than I saw that something had happened since the morning. She was leaning back on her bench, her hands were clasped in her lap, and her eyes were fixed upon the landlady, at the other side of the court, manipulating her apricots.

But I saw she was not thinking of apricots She was staring absently, thoughtfully; as I came near her I perceived that she had been crying. I sat down on the bench beside her before she saw me; then, when she had done so, she simply turned round, without surprise, and rested her sad eyes upon me. Something very bad indeed had happened; she was completely changed.

I immediately charged her with it. 'Your cousin has been giving you bad news; you are in great distress.'

For a moment she said nothing, and I supposed that she was afraid to speak, lest her tears should come back. But presently I perceived that in the short time that had elapsed since my leaving her in the morning she had shed them all, and that she was now softly stoical – intensely composed.

'My poor cousin is in distress,' she said at last. 'His news was bad.' Then, after a brief hesitation – 'He was in terrible want of money.'

'In want of yours, you mean?'

'Of any that he could get – honestly. Mine was the only money.'

'And he has taken yours?'

She hesitated again a moment, but her glance, meanwhile, was pleading. 'I gave him what I had.'

I have always remembered the accent of those words as the most angelic bit of human utterance I had ever listened to; but then, almost with a sense of personal outrage, I jumped up. 'Good heavens!' I said, 'do you call that getting it honestly?'

I had gone too far; she blushed deeply. 'We will not speak of it,' she said.

'We *must* speak of it,' I answered, sitting down again. 'I am your friend; it seems to me you need one. What is the matter with your cousin?'

'He is in debt.'

'No doubt! But what is the special fitness of your paying his debts?'

'He has told me all his story; I am very sorry for him.'

'So am I! But I hope he will give you back your money.'

'Certainly he will; as soon as he can.'

'When will that be?'

'When he has finished his great picture.'

'My dear young lady, confound his great picture! Where is this desperate cousin?'

She certainly hesitated now. Then – 'At his dinner,' she answered.

I turned about and looked through the open door into the *salle à manger*. There, alone at the end of a long table, I perceived the object of Miss Spencer's compassion – the bright young art-student. He was dining too attentively to notice me at first; but in the act of setting down a well-emptied wine-glass he caught sight of my observant attitude. He paused in his repast, and, with his head on one side and his meagre jaws slowly moving, fixedly returned my gaze. Then the landlady came lightly brushing by with her pyramid of apricots.

'And that nice little plate of fruit is for him?' I exclaimed.

Miss Spencer glanced at it tenderly 'They do that so prettily!' she murmured.

I felt helpless and irritated. 'Come now, really,' I said; 'do you approve of that long strong fellow accepting your funds?' She looked away from me; I was evidently giving her pain. The case was hopeless; the long strong fellow had 'interested' her.

'Excuse me if I speak of him so unceremoniously,' I said. 'But you are really too generous, and he is not quite delicate enough. He made his debts himself – he ought to pay them himself.'

'He has been foolish,' she answered; 'I know that. He has told me everything. We had a long talk this morning; the poor fellow threw himself upon my charity. He has signed notes to a large amount.'

'The more fool he!'

'He is in extreme distress; and it is not only himself. It is his poor wife.'

'Ah, he has a poor wife?'

'I didn't know it – but he confessed everything. He married two years since, secretly.'

'Why secretly?'

Caroline Spencer glanced about her, as if she feared listeners. Then softly, in a little impressive tone – 'She was a Countess!'

'Are you very sure of that?'

'She has written me a most beautiful letter.'

'Asking you for money, eh?'

'Asking me for confidence and sympathy,' said Miss Spencer. 'She has been disinherited by her father. My cousin told me the story, and she tells it in her own way, in the letter. It is like an old romance. Her father opposed the marriage, and when he discovered that she had secretly disobeyed him he cruelly cast her off. It is really most romantic. They are the oldest family in Provence.'

I looked and listened in wonder. It really seemed that the poor woman was enjoying the 'romance' of having a discarded Countess-cousin, out of Provence, so deeply as almost to lose the sense of what the forfeiture of her money meant for her.

'My dear young lady,' I said, 'you don't want to be ruined for picturesqueness' sake?'

'I shall not be ruined. I shall come back before long to stay with them. The Countess insists upon that.'

'Come back! You are going home, then?'

She sat for a moment with her eyes lowered, then with an heroic suppression of a faint tremor of the voice – 'I have no money for travelling!' she answered.

'You gave it *all* up?'

'I have kept enough to take me home.'

I gave an angry groan, and at this juncture Miss Spencer's cousin, the fortunate possessor of her sacred savings and of the hand of the Provençal Countess, emerged from the little dining-room. He stood on the threshold for an instant, removing the stone from a plump apricot which he had brought away from the table; then he put the apricot into his mouth, and while he let it sojourn there, gratefully, stood looking at us, with his long legs apart and his hands dropped into the pockets of his velvet jacket. My companion got up, giving him a thin glance which I caught in its passage, and which expressed a strange commixture of resignation and fascination – a sort of perverted exaltation. Ugly, vulgar, pretentious, dishonest, as I thought the creature, he had appealed successfully to her eager and tender imagination. I was deeply disgusted, but I had no warrant to interfere, and at any rate I felt that it would be vain.

The young man waved his hand with a pictorial gesture. 'Nice old court,' he observed. 'Nice mellow old place. Good tone in that brick. Nice crooked old staircase.'

Decidedly, I couldn't stand it; without responding I gave my hand to Caroline Spencer. She looked at me an instant with her little white face and expanded eyes, and as she showed her pretty teeth I suppose she meant to smile.

'Don't be sorry for me,' she said, 'I am very sure I shall see something of this dear old Europe yet.'

I told her that I would not bid her good-bye – I should find a moment to come back the next morning. Her cousin, who had put on his sombrero again, flourished it off at me by way of a bow – upon which I took my departure.

The next morning I came back to the inn, where I met in the court the landlady, more loosely laced than in the evening. On my asking for Miss Spencer, – 'Partie, monsieur,' said the hostess. 'She went away last night at ten o'clock, with her – her – not her husband, eh? – in fine, her Monsieur. They went down to the American ship.' I turned away; the poor girl had been about thirteen hours in Europe.

Chapter 4

I MYSELF, MORE FORTUNATE, was there some five years longer. During this period I lost my friend Latouche, who died of a malarious fever during a tour in the Levant. One of the first things I did on my return was to go up to Grimwinter to pay a consolatory visit to his poor mother. I found her in deep affliction, and I sat with her the whole of the morning that followed my arrival (I had come in late at night), listening to her tearful descant and singing the praises of my friend. We talked of nothing else, and our conversation terminated only with the arrival of a quick little woman who drove herself up to the door in a 'carry-all,' and whom I saw toss the reins upon the horse's back with the briskness of a startled sleeper throwing back the bed-clothes. She jumped out of the carry-all and she jumped into the room. She proved to be the minister's wife and the great town gossip, and she had evidently, in the latter capacity, a choice morsel to communicate. I was as sure of this as I was that poor Mrs Latouche was not absolutely too bereaved to listen to her. It seemed to me discreet to retire, I said I believed I would go and take a walk before dinner.

'And, by the way,' I added, 'if you will tell me where my old friend Miss Spencer lives, I will walk to her house.'

The minister's wife immediately responded. Miss Spencer lived in the fourth house beyond the Baptist church; the Baptist church was the one on the right, with that queer green thing over the door; they called it a portico, but it looked more like an old-fashioned bedstead.

'Yes, do go and see poor Caroline,' said Mrs Latouche. 'It will refresh her to see a strange face.'

'I should think she had had enough of strange faces!' cried the minister's wife.

'I mean, to see a visitor,' said Mrs Latouche, amending her phrase.

'I should think she had had enough of visitors!' her companion rejoined. 'But *you* don't mean to stay ten years,' she added, glancing at me.

'Has she a visitor of that sort?' I inquired, perplexed.

'You will see the sort!' said the minister's wife. 'She's easily seen; she generally sits in the front yard. Only take care what you say to her, and be very sure you are polite.'

'Ah, she is so sensitive?'

The minister's wife jumped up and dropped me a curtsey – a most ironical curtsey.

'That's what she is, if you please. She's a Countess!'

And pronouncing this word with the most scathing accent, the little woman seemed fairly to laugh in the Countess's face. I stood a moment, staring, wondering, remembering.

'Oh, I shall be very polite!' I cried; and grasping my hat and stick, I went on my way.

I found Miss Spencer's residence without difficulty. The Baptist church was easily identified, and the small dwelling near it, of a rusty white, with a large central chimney-stack and a Virginia creeper, seemed naturally and properly the abode of a frugal old maid with a taste for the picturesque. As I approached I slackened my pace, for I had heard that some one was always sitting in the front yard, and I wished to reconnoitre. I looked cautiously over the low white fence which separated the small garden-space from the unpaved street; but I descried nothing in the shape of a Countess. A small straight path led up to the crooked door-step, and on either side of it was a little grass-plot, fringed with currant-bushes. In the middle of the grass, on either side, was a large quince-tree, full of antiquity and contortions, and beneath one of the quince-trees were placed a small table and a couple of chairs. On the table lay a piece of unfinished embroidery and two or three books in bright-coloured paper covers. I went in at the gate and paused halfway along the path, scanning the place for some farther token of its occupant, before whom – I could hardly have said why – I hesitated abruptly to present myself. Then I saw that the poor little house was very shabby. I felt a sudden doubt of my right to intrude; for curiosity had been my motive, and curiosity here seemed singularly indelicate. While I hesitated, a figure appeared in the open doorway and stood there looking at me. I immediately recognised Caroline Spencer, but she looked at me as if she had never seen me before. Gently, but gravely and timidly, I advanced to the door-step, and then I said, with an attempt at friendly badinage –

'I waited for you over there to come back, but you never came.'

'Waited where, sir?' she asked softly, and her light-coloured eyes expanded more than before.

She was much older; she looked tired and wasted.

'Well,' I said, 'I waited at Havre.'

She stared; then she recognised me. She smiled and blushed and clasped her two hands together. 'I remember you now,' she said. 'I remember that day.' But she stood there, neither coming out nor asking me to come in. She was embarrassed.

I, too, felt a little awkward. I poked my stick into the path. 'I kept looking out for you, year after year,' I said.

'You mean in Europe?' murmured Miss Spencer.

'In Europe, of course! Here, apparently, you are easy enough to find.'

She leaned her hand against the unpainted door-post, and her head fell a little to one side. She looked at me for a moment without speaking, and I thought I recognised the expression that one sees in women's eyes when tears are rising. Suddenly she stepped out upon the cracked slab of stone before the threshold and closed the door behind her. Then she began to smile intently, and I saw that her teeth were as pretty as ever. But there had been tears too.

'Have you been there ever since?' she asked, almost in a whisper.

'Until three weeks ago. And you – you never came back?'

Still looking at me with her fixed smile, she put her hand behind her and opened the door again. 'I am not very polite,' she said. 'Won't you come in?'

'I am afraid I incommode you.'

'Oh no!' she answered, smiling more than ever. And she pushed back the door, with a sign that I should enter.

I went in, following her. She led the way to a small room on the left of the narrow hall, which I supposed to be her parlour, though it was at the back of the house, and we passed the closed door of another apartment which apparently enjoyed a view of the quince-trees. This one looked out upon a small wood-shed and two clucking hens. But I thought it very pretty, until I saw that its elegance was of the most frugal kind; after which, presently, I thought it prettier still, for I had never seen faded chintz and old mezzotint engravings, framed in varnished autumn leaves, disposed in so graceful a fashion. Miss Spencer sat down on a very small portion of the sofa, with her hands tightly clasped in her lap. She looked ten years older, and it would have sounded very perverse now to speak of her as pretty. But I thought her so; or at least I thought her touching. She was peculiarly agitated. I tried to appear not to notice it; but suddenly, in the most inconsequent fashion – it was an irresistible memory of our little friendship at Havre – I said to her – 'I do incommode you. You are distressed.'

She raised her two hands to her face, and for a moment kept it buried in them. Then, taking them away – 'It's because you remind me . . .' she said.

'I remind you, you mean, of that miserable day at Havre?'

She shook her head. 'It was not miserable. It was delightful.'

'I never was so shocked as when, on going back to your inn the next morning, I found you had set sail again.'

She was silent a moment; and then she said – 'Please let us not speak of that.'

'Did you come straight back here?' I asked.

'I was back here just thirty days after I had gone away.'

'And here you have remained ever since?'

'Oh yes!' she said, gently.

'When are you going to Europe again?'

This question seemed brutal; but there was something that irritated me in the softness of her resignation, and I wished to extort from her some expression of impatience.

She fixed her eyes for a moment upon a small sunspot on the carpet, then she got up and lowered the window blind a little, to obliterate it.

Presently, in the same mild voice, answering my question, she said – 'Never!'

'I hope your cousin repaid you your money.'

'I don't care for it now,' she said, looking away from me.

'You don't care for your money?'

'For going to Europe.'

'Do you mean that you would not go if you could?'

'I can't – I can't,' said Caroline Spencer. 'It is all over; I never think of it.'

'He never repaid you, then!' I exclaimed.

'Please – please,' she began.

But she stopped; she was looking toward the door. There had been a rustling and a sound of steps in the hall.

I also looked toward the door, which was open, and now admitted another person – a lady who paused just within the threshold. Behind her came a young man. The lady looked at me with a good deal of fixedness – long enough for my glance to receive a vivid impression of herself. Then she turned to Caroline Spencer, and, with a smile and a strong foreign accent –

'Excuse my interruption!' she said. 'I knew not you had company – the gentleman came in so quietly.'

With this she directed her eyes toward me again.

She was very strange: yet my first feeling was that I had seen her before. Then I perceived that I had only seen ladies who were very much like her. But I had seen them very far away from Grimwinter, and it was an odd sensation to be seeing her here. Whither was it the sight of her seemed to transport me! To some dusky landing before a shabby Parisian *quatrième* – to an open door revealing a greasy ante-chamber, and to Madame leaning over the banisters while she holds a faded dressing-gown together and bawls down to the portress to bring up her coffee. Miss Spencer's visitor was a very large woman, of middle age with a plump dead-white face, and hair drawn back *à la chinoise*. She had a small penetrating eye, and what is called in French an agreeable smile. She wore an old pink cashmere dressing-gown covered with white embroideries, and, like the figure in my momentary vision, she was holding it together in front with a bare and rounded arm and a plump and deeply-dimpled hand.

'It is only to spick about my *café*,' she said to Miss Spencer, with her agreeable smile. 'I should like it served in the garden under the leetle tree.'

The young man behind her had now stepped into the room, and he also stood looking at me. He was a pretty-faced little fellow, with an air of provincial foppishness – a tiny Adonis of Grimwinter. He had a small pointed nose, a small pointed chin, and, as I observed, the most diminutive feet. He looked at me foolishly, with his mouth open.

'You shall have your coffee,' said Miss Spencer, who had a faint red spot in each of her cheeks.

'It is well!' said the lady in the dressing-gown. 'Find your book,' she added, turning to the young man.

He looked vaguely round the room. 'My grammar, d'ye mean?' he asked, with a helpless intonation.

But the large lady was looking at me curiously, and gathering in her dressing-gown with her white arm.

'Find your book, my friend,' she repeated.

'My poetry, d'ye mean?' said the young man, also gazing at me again.

'Never mind your book,' said his companion. 'Today we will talk. We will make some conversation. But we must not interrupt. Come,' and she turned away. 'Under the leetle tree,' she added, for the benefit of Miss Spencer.

Then she gave me a sort of salutation, and a 'Monsieur!' – With which she swept away again, followed by the young man.

Caroline Spencer stood there with her eyes fixed upon the ground.

'Who is that?' I asked.

'The Countess, my cousin.'

'And who is the young man?'

'Her pupil, Mr Mixter.'

This description of the relation between the two persons who had just left the room made me break into a little laugh. Miss Spencer looked at me gravely.

'She gives French lessons; she has lost her fortune.'

'I see,' I said. 'She is determined to be a burden to no one. That is very proper.'

Miss Spencer looked down on the ground again. 'I must go and get the coffee,' she said.

'Has the lady many pupils?' I asked.

'She has only Mr Mixter. She gives all her time to him.'

At this I could not laugh, though I smelt provocation. Miss Spencer was too grave. 'He pays very well,' she presently added, with simplicity. 'He is very rich. He is very kind. He takes the Countess to drive.' And she was turning away.

'You are going for the Countess's coffee?' I said.

'If you will excuse me a few moments.'

'Is there no one else to do it?'

She looked at me with the softest serenity. 'I keep no servants.'

'Can she not wait upon herself?'

'She is not used to that.'

'I see,' said I, as gently as possible. 'But before you go, tell me this: who is this lady?'

'I told you about her before – that day. She is the wife of my cousin, whom you saw.'

'The lady who was disowned by her family in consequence of her marriage?'

'Yes; they have never seen her again. They have cast her off.'

'And where is her husband?'

'He is dead.'

'And where is your money?'

The poor girl flinched, there was something too methodical in my questions. 'I don't know,' she said wearily.

But I continued a moment. 'On her husband's death this lady came over here?'

'Yes, she arrived one day.'

'How long ago?'

'Two years.'

'She has been here ever since?'

'Every moment.'

'How does she like it?'

'Not at all.'

'And how do *you* like it?'

Miss Spencer laid her face in her two hands an instant, as she had done ten minutes before. Then, quickly, she went to get the Countess's coffee.

I remained alone in the little parlour; I wanted to see more – to learn more. At the end of five minutes the young man whom Miss Spencer had described as the Countess's pupil came in. He stood looking at me for a moment with parted lips. I saw he was a very rudimentary young man.

'She wants to know if you won't come out there?" he observed at last.

'Who wants to know?'

'The Countess. That French lady.'

'She has asked you to bring me?'

'Yes, sir,' said the young man feebly, looking at my six feet of stature.

I went out with him and we found the Countess sitting under one of the little quince-trees in front of the house. She was drawing a needle through the piece of embroidery which she had taken from the small table. She pointed graciously to the chair beside her and I seated myself. Mr Mixter glanced about him, and then sat down in the grass at her feet. He gazed upward, looking with parted lips from the Countess to me.

'I am sure you speak French,' said the Countess, fixing her brilliant little eyes upon me.

'I do, madam, after a fashion,' I answered in the lady's own tongue.

'*Voilà!*' she cried most expressively. 'I knew it so soon as I looked at you. You have been in my poor dear country.'

'A long time.'

'You know Paris?'

'Thoroughly, madam.' And with a certain conscious purpose I let my eyes meet her own.

She presently, hereupon, moved her own and glanced down at Mr Mixter. 'What are we talking about?' she demanded of her attentive pupil.

He pulled his knees up, plucked at the grass with his hand, stared, blushed a little. 'You are talking French,' said Mr Mixter.

'*La belle découverte!*' said the Countess. 'Here are ten months,' she explained to me, 'that I am giving him lessons. Don't put yourself out not to say he's a fool; he won't understand you.'

'I hope your other pupils are more gratifying,' I remarked.

'I have no others. They don't know what French is in this place; they don't want to know. You may therefore imagine the pleasure it is to me to meet a person who speaks it like yourself.' I replied that my own pleasure was not less, and she went on drawing her stitches through her embroidery, with her little finger curled out. Every few moments she put her eyes close to her work, near-sightedly. I thought her a very disagreeable person; she was coarse, affected, dishonest, and no more a Countess than I was a caliph. 'Talk to me of Paris,' she went on. 'The very name of it gives me an emotion! How long since you were there?'

'Two months ago.'

'Happy man! Tell me something about it. What were they doing? Oh, for an hour of the boulevard!'

'They were doing about what they are always doing – amusing themselves a good deal.'

'At the theatres, eh?' sighed the Countess. 'At the *cafés-concerts* – at the little tables in front of the doors? *Quelle existence!* You know I am a Parisienne, Monsieur,' she added, ' – to my finger-tips.'

'Miss Spencer was mistaken, then,' I ventured to rejoin, 'in telling me that you are a Provençale.'

She stared a moment, then she put her nose to her embroidery, which had a dingy, desultory aspect. 'Ah, I am a Provençale by birth; but I am a Parisienne by – inclination.'

'And by experience, I suppose?' I said.

She questioned me a moment with her hard little eyes. 'Oh, experience! I could talk of experience. If I wished. I never expected, for example, that experience had *this* in store for me.' And she pointed with her bare elbow, and with a jerk of her head – at everything that surrounded her – at the little white house, the quince-tree, the rickety paling, even at Mr Mixter.

'You are in exile!' I said, smiling.

'You may imagine what it is! These two years that I have been here I have passed hours – hours! One gets used to things, and sometimes I think I have got used to this. But there are some things that are always beginning over again. For example, my coffee.'

'Do you always have coffee at this hour?' I inquired.

She tossed back her head and measured me.

'At what hour would you prefer me to have it? I must have my little cup after breakfast.'

'Ah, you breakfast at this hour?'

'At mid-day – *comme cela se fait*. Here they breakfast at a quarter past seven! That "quarter past" is charming!'

'But you were telling me about your coffee,' I observed, sympathetically.

'My *cousine* can't believe in it; she can't understand it. She's an excellent girl; but that little cup of black coffee, with a drop of cognac, served at this hour – they exceed her comprehension. So I have to break the ice every day, and it takes the coffee the time you see to arrive. And when it arrives, Monsieur! If I don't offer you any of it you must not take it ill. It will be because I know you have drunk it on the boulevard.'

I resented extremely this scornful treatment of poor Caroline Spencer's humble hospitality; but I said nothing, in order to say nothing uncivil. I only looked on Mr Mixter, who had clasped his arms round his knees and was watching my companion's demonstrative graces in solemn fascination. She presently saw that I was observing him; she glanced at me with a little bold explanatory smile. 'You know, he adores me,' she murmured, putting her nose into her tapestry again. I expressed the promptest credence, and she went on. 'He dreams of becoming my lover! Yes, it's his dream. He has read a French novel; it took him six months. But ever since that he has thought himself the hero, and me the heroine!'

Mr Mixter had evidently not an idea that he was being talked about; he was too preoccupied with the ecstasy of contemplation. At this moment Caroline Spencer came out of the house, bearing a coffee-pot on a little tray. I noticed that on her way from the door to the table she gave me a single quick, vaguely-appealing glance. I wondered what it signified; I felt that it signified a sort of half-frightened longing to know what, as a man of the world who had been in France, I thought of the Countess. It made me extremely uncomfortable. I could not tell her that the Countess was very possibly the runaway wife of a little hair-dresser. I tried suddenly, on the contrary, to show a high consideration for her. But I got up; I couldn't stay longer. It vexed me to see Caroline Spencer standing there like a waiting-maid.

'You expect to remain some time at Grimwinter?' I said to the Countess.

She gave a terrible shrug.

'Who knows? Perhaps for years. When one is in misery! . . . *Chère belle*,' she added, turning to Miss Spencer, 'you have forgotten the cognac!'

I detained Caroline Spencer as, after looking a moment in silence at the little table, she was turning away to procure this missing delicacy. I silently gave her my hand in farewell. She looked very tired, but there was a strange hint of prospective patience in her severely mild little face. I thought she was rather glad I was going. Mr Mixter had risen to his feet and was pouring out the Countess's coffee. As I went back past the Baptist church I reflected that poor Miss Spencer had been right in her presentiment that she should still see something of that dear old Europe.

LONGSTAFF'S MARRIAGE

FORTY YEARS AGO that traditional and anecdotical liberty of young American women which is notoriously the envy and despair of their foreign sisters was not so firmly established as at the present hour; yet it was sufficiently recognised to make it no scandal that so pretty a girl as Diana Belfield should start for the grand tour of Europe under no more imposing protection than that of her cousin and intimate friend, Miss Agatha Josling. She had, from the European point of view, beauty enough to make her enterprise perilous – the beauty foreshadowed in her name, which might have been given in provision of her tall light figure, her nobly poised head weighted with a coronal of auburn braids, her frank quick glance, and her rapid gliding step. She used often to walk about with a big dog, who had the habit of bounding at her side and tossing his head against her outstretched hand; and she had, moreover, a trick of carrying her long parasol always folded, for she was not afraid of the sunshine, across her shoulder, in the fashion of a soldier's musket on a march. Thus equipped, she looked wonderfully like that charming antique statue of the goddess of the chase which we encounter in various replicas in half the museums of the world. You half expected to see a sandal-shod foot peep out beneath her fluttering robe. It was with this tread of the wakeful huntress that she stepped upon the old sailing-vessel which was to bear her to foreign lands. Behind her with a great many shawls and satchels, came her little kinswoman, with quite another *démarche*. Agatha Josling was not a beauty, but she was the most judicious and most devoted of companions. These two persons had been united by the death of Diana's mother, when the latter young lady took possession of her patrimony. The first use she made of her inheritance was to divide it with Agatha, who had not a penny of her own; the next was to purchase a letter of credit upon a European banker. The cousins had contracted a classical friendship – they had determined to be all in all to each other like the Ladies of Llangollen. Only, though their friendship was exclusive, their Llangollen was to be comprehensive. They would tread the pavements of historic cities and wander through the aisles of Gothic cathedrals, wind on tinkling mules through mountain gorges and sit among dark eyed peasants on the shores of blue lakes. It may seem singular that a beautiful girl with a pretty fortune should have been left to seek the supreme satisfaction of life in friendship tempered by sight-seeing; but Diana herself considered this pastime no beggarly alternative. Though she never told it herself, her biographer may do so; she had had, in vulgar parlance, a hundred offers. To say that she had declined them is to say too little; they had filled her with contempt. They had come from honourable and amiable men, and it was not her suitors in themselves that she contemned; it was simply the idea of marrying. She found it insupportable; a fact which completes her analogy with the mythic divinity to whom I have likened her. She was passionately single, fiercely virginal; and in the straight-glancing gray eye which provoked men to admire, there was a certain silvery ray which forbade them to hope. The fabled Diana took a fancy to a beautiful shepherd, but the real one had not yet found, sleeping or waking, her Endymion.

Thanks to this defensive eyebeam, the dangerous side of our heroine's enterprise was slow to define itself thanks, too, to the exquisite propriety of her companion. Agatha Josling had an almost Quakerish purity and dignity; a bristling dragon could not have been a better safeguard than this glossy, gray-breasted dove. Money, too, is a protection, and Diana had money enough to purchase privacy. She travelled largely, and saw all the churches and pictures, the castles and cottages, included in the list which had been drawn up by the two friends in evening talks at home, between two wax candles. In the evening they used to read aloud to each other from *Corinne* and *Childe Harold*, and they kept a diary in common, at which they 'collaborated,' like French playwrights, and which was studded with quotations from the authors I have mentioned. This lasted a year, at the end of which they found themselves a trifle weary. A snug posting-carriage was a delightful habitation, but looking at miles of pictures was very fatiguing to the back. Buying souvenirs and trinkets under foreign arcades was a most absorbing occupation; but inns were dreadfully apt to be draughty, and bottles of hot water for application to the feet, had a disagreeable way of growing lukewarm. For these and other reasons our heroines determined to take a winter's rest, and for this purpose they betook themselves to the charming town of Nice, which was then but in the infancy of its fame. It was simply one of the hundred hamlets of the Riviera – a place where the blue waves broke on an almost empty strand and the olive-trees sprouted at the doors of the inns. In those days Nice was Italian, and the 'Promenade des Anglais' existed only in an embryonic form. Exist, however, it did, practically, and British invalids, in moderate numbers, might have been seen taking the January sunshine beneath London umbrellas before the many-twinkling sea.

Our young Americans quietly took their place in this harmless society. They drove along the coast, through the strange, dark, huddled fishing villages, and they rode on donkeys among the bosky hills. They painted in water-colours and hired a piano; they subscribed to the circulating library, and took lessons in the language of Silvio Pellico from an old lady with very fine eyes, who wore an enormous brooch of cracked malachite, and gave herself out as the widow of a Roman exile.

They used to go and sit by the sea, each provided with a volume from the circulating library; but they never did much with their books. The sunshine made the page too dazzling, and the people who strolled up and down before them were more entertaining than the ladies and gentlemen in the novels. They looked at them constantly from under their umbrellas; they learned to know them all by sight. Many of their fellow-visitors were invalids – mild, slow-moving consumptives. But for the fact that women enjoy the exercise of pity, I should have said that these pale promenaders were a saddening spectacle. In several of them, however, our friends took a personal interest; they watched them from day to day; they noticed their changing colour; they had their ideas about who was getting better and who was getting worse. They did little, however, in the way of making acquaintances – partly because pulmonary sufferers are no great talkers, and partly because this was also Diana's disposition. She said to her friend that they had not come to Europe to pay morning-calls; they had left their best bonnets and card-cases behind them. At the bottom of her reserve was the apprehension that she should be 'admired;' which was not fatuity, but simply an induction from an embarrassing experience. She had seen in Europe, for the first time, certain horrid men – polished adventurers with offensive looks and mercenary thoughts; and she had a wholesome fear that one of these gentlemen might approach her through some accidental breach in her reserve. Agatha Josling, who had neither in reminiscence nor in prospect the same reasons for turning her graceful back, would have been glad to extend the circle of their acquaintance, and would even have consented to put on her best bonnet for the purpose. But she had to content herself with an occasional murmur of small-talk, on a bench before the sea, with two or three English ladies of the botanising class; jovial little spinsters who wore stout boots, gauntlets, and 'uglies,' and in pursuit of wayside flowers scrambled into places where the first-mentioned articles were uncompromisingly visible. For the rest, Agatha contented herself with spinning suppositions about the people she never spoke to. She framed a great deal of hypothetic gossip, invented theories and explanations – generally of the most charitable quality. Her companion took no part in these harmless devisings, except to listen to them with an indolent smile. She seldom honoured her fellow-mortals with finding apologies for them, and if they wished her to read their history they must write it out in the largest letters.

There was one person at Nice upon whose biography, if it had been laid before her in this fashion, she probably would have bestowed a certain amount of attention. Agatha had noticed the gentleman first; or Agatha, at least, had first spoken of him. He was young and he looked interesting; Agatha had indulged in a good deal of wondering as to whether or no he belonged to the invalid category. She preferred to believe that one of his lungs was 'affected;' it certainly made him more interesting. He used to stroll about by himself and sit for a long time in the sun, with a book peeping out of his pocket. This book he never opened; he was always staring at the sea. I say always, but my phrase demands an immediate modification; he looked at the sea, whenever he was not looking at Diana Belfield. He was tall and fair, slight, and, as Agatha Josling said, aristocratic-looking. He dressed with a certain careless elegance which Agatha a deemed picturesque; she declared one day that he reminded her of a love-sick prince. She learned eventually from one of the botanising spinsters that he was not a prince, that he was simply an English gentleman, Mr Reginald Longstaff. There remained the possibility that he was love sick; but this point could not be so easily settled. Agatha's informant had assured her, however, that if they were not princes, the Longstaffs, who came from a part of the country in which she had visited, and owned great estates there, had a pedigree which many princes might envy. It was one of the oldest and the best of English names, they were one of the innumerable untitled country families who held their heads as high as the highest. This poor Mr Longstaff was a beautiful specimen of a young English gentleman; he looked so gentle, yet so brave; so modest, yet so cultivated! The ladies spoke of him habitually as 'poor' Mr Longstaff, for they now took for granted that there was something the matter with him. At last Agatha Josling discovered what it was, and made a solemn proclamation of the same. The matter with poor Mr Longstaff was simply that he was in love with Diana! It was certainly natural to suppose he was in love with some one, and, as Agatha said, it could not possibly be with herself. Mr Longstaff was pale and slightly dishevelled; he never spoke to any one, he was evidently preoccupied, and his mild, candid face was a sufficient proof that the weight on his heart was not a bad conscience. What could it be, then but an unrequited passion? It was, however, equally pertinent to inquire why Mr Longstaff took no steps to bring about a requital.

'Why in the world does he not ask to be introduced to you?' Agatha Josling demanded of her companion.

Diana replied, quite without eagerness, that it was plainly because he had nothing to say to her; and she declared with a trifle more emphasis that she was incapable of proposing to him a topic of conversation. She added that she thought they had gossiped enough about the poor man, and that if by any chance he should have the bad taste to speak to them, she would certainly go away and leave him alone with Miss Josling. It is true, however, that at an earlier period she had let fall the remark that he was quite the most 'distinguished' person at Nice; and afterwards, though she was never the first to allude to him, she had more than once let her companion pursue the theme for some time without reminding her of its futility. The one person to whom Mr Longstaff was observed to speak was an elderly man of foreign aspect, who approached him occasionally in the most deferential manner, and whom Agatha Josling supposed to be his servant. This individual was apparently an Italian; he had an obsequious attitude, a pair of grizzled whiskers, an insinuating smile. He seemed to come to Mr Longstaff for orders; presently he went away to execute them, and Agatha noticed that on retiring he always managed to pass in front of her companion, on whom he fixed his respectful, but penetrating gaze. 'He knows the secret,' she always said, with gentle jocoseness; 'he knows what is the matter with his master, and he wants to see whether he approves of you. Old servants never want their masters to marry, and I think this worthy man is rather afraid of you. At any rate, the way he stares at you tells the whole story.'

'Every one stares at me!' said Diana, wearily. 'A cat may look at a king.'

As the weeks went by Agatha Josling quite made up her mind that Mr Longstaff's complaint was pulmonary. The poor young man's invalid character was now quite apparent; he could hardly hold up his head or drag one foot after the other; his servant was always near him to give him an arm or to hand him an extra overcoat. No one indeed knew with certainty that he was consumptive but Agatha agreed with the lady who had given the information about his pedigree, that this fact was in itself extremely suspicious; for, as the little Englishwoman forcibly remarked, unless he were ill, why should he make such a mystery of it? Consumption declaring itself in a young man of family and fortune was particularly sad; such people often had diplomatic reasons for pretending to enjoy excellent health. It kept the legacy-hunters and the hungry next-of-kin from worrying them to death. Agatha observed that this poor gentleman's last hours seemed likely to be only too lonely. She felt very much like offering to nurse him, for, being no relation, he could not accuse her of mercenary motives. From time to time he got up from the bench where he habitually sat, and strolled slowly past the two friends. Every time that he came near them Agatha had a singular feeling – a conviction that now he was really going to speak to them. He would speak with the gravest courtesy – she could not fancy him speaking otherwise. He began, at a distance, by fixing his grave, soft eyes on Diana, and as he advanced you would have said that he was coming straight up to her with some tremulous compliment. But as he drew nearer his intentness seemed to falter; he strolled more slowly, he looked away at the sea, and he passed in front of her without having the courage to let his eyes rest upon her. Then he passed back again in the same fashion, sank down upon his bench, fatigued apparently by his aimless stroll, and fell into a melancholy reverie. To enumerate these accidents is to attribute to his behaviour a certain aggressiveness which it was far from possessing; there was something scrupulous and subdued in his manner which made it perfectly discreet, and it may be affirmed that not a single idler on the sunny shore suspected his speechless 'attentions.'

'I wonder why it doesn't annoy us more that he should look at us so much,' said Agatha Josling one day.

'That who should look at us?' asked Diana, not at all affectedly.

Agatha fixed her eyes for a moment on her friend, and then said gently –

'Mr Longstaff. Now, don't say, "Who is Mr Longstaff?" ' she added.

'I have yet to learn, really,' said Diana, 'that the person you appear to mean does look at us. I have never caught him in the act.'

'That is because whenever you turn your eyes towards him he looks away. He is afraid to meet them. But I see him.'

These words were exchanged one day as the two friends sat as usual before the twinkling sea; and beyond them, as usual, lounged Reginald Longstaff. Diana bent her head faintly forward and glanced towards him. He was looking full at her, and their eyes met, apparently for the first time. Diana dropped her own upon her book again, and then, after a silence of some moments, 'It does annoy me,' she said. Presently she added that she would go home and write a letter, and, though she had never taken a step in Europe without having Agatha by her side, Miss Josling now allowed her to depart unattended. 'You won't mind going alone?' Agatha had asked. 'It is but three minutes, you know.'

Diana replied that she preferred to go alone, and she moved away, with her parasol over her shoulder.

Agatha Josling had a particular reason for this variation from their maidenly custom. She felt a sudden conviction that if she were left alone Mr Longstaff would come and speak to her, and say something very important, and she accommodated herself to this conviction without the sense of doing anything immodest. There was something solemn about it; it was a sort of presentiment; but it did not frighten her; it only made her feel very kind and appreciative. It is true that when at the end of ten minutes (they had seemed rather long), she saw the young man rise from his seat and slowly come towards her, she was conscious of a certain trepidation. Mr Longstaff drew near; at last he was close to her; he stopped and stood looking at her. She had averted her head, so as not to appear to expect him; but now she looked round again, and he very gravely lifted his hat.

'May I take the liberty of sitting down?' he asked.

Agatha bowed in silence and, to make room for him moved a certain blue shawl of Diana's, which was lying on the bench. He slowly sank into the place, and then said very gently –

'I have ventured to speak to you, because I have something particular to say.' His voice trembled, and he was extremely pale. His eyes, which Agatha thought very handsome, had a remarkable expression.

'I am afraid you are ill,' she said, with great kindness. 'I have often noticed you and pitied you.'

'I thought you did, a little,' the young man answered. 'That is why I made up my mind to speak to you.'

'You are getting worse,' said Agatha, softly.

'Yes, I am getting worse; I am dying. I am perfectly conscious of it; I have no illusions. I am weaker every day; I shall last but a few weeks.' This was said very simply; sadly, but not lugubriously.

But Agatha felt almost awe-stricken; there stirred in her heart a delicate sense of sisterhood with this beautiful young man who sat there and talked so submissively of death.

'Can nothing be done?' she said.

He shook his head and smiled a little. 'Nothing but to try and get what pleasure I can from this little remnant of life.'

Though he smiled she felt that he was very serious; that he was, indeed, deeply agitated, and trying to master his emotion.

'I am afraid you get very little pleasure,' Agatha rejoined. 'You seem entirely alone.'

'I am entirely alone. I have no family – no near relations. I am absolutely alone.'

Agatha rested her eyes on him compassionately, and then –

'You ought to have spoken to us,' she said.

He sat looking at her; he had taken off his hat; he was slowly passing his hand over his forehead. 'You see I do – at last!'

'You wanted to before?'

'Very often.'

'I thought so!' said Agatha, with a candour which was in itself a dignity.

'But I couldn't,' said Mr Longstaff. 'I never saw you alone.'

Before she knew it Agatha was blushing a little; for, to the ear, simply, his words implied that it was to her only he would have addressed himself for the pleasure he had coveted. But the next instant she had become conscious that what he meant was simply that he admired her companion so much that he was afraid of her, and that, daring to speak to herself, he thought her a much less formidable and less interesting personage. Her blush immediately faded; for there was no resentment to keep the colour in her cheek; and there was no resentment still when she perceived that, though her neighbour was looking straight at her, with his inspired, expanded eyes, he was thinking too much of Diana to have noticed this little play of confusion.

'Yes, it's very true,' she said. 'It is the first time my friend has left me.'

'She is very beautiful,' said Mr Longstaff.

'Very beautiful – and as good as she is beautiful.'

'Yes, yes,' he rejoined, solemnly. 'I am sure of that. I *know* it!'

'I know it even better than you,' said Agatha, smiling a little.

'Then you will have all the more patience with what I want to say to you. It is very strange; it will make you think, at first, that I am perhaps out of my mind. But I am not, I am thoroughly reasonable. You will see.' Then he paused a moment; his voice had begun to tremble again.

'I know what you are going to say,' said Agatha, very gently. 'You are in love with my friend.'

Mr Longstaff gave her a look of devoted gratitude; he lifted up the edge of the blue shawl which he had often seen Diana wear, and pressed it to his lips.

'I am extremely grateful!' he exclaimed. 'You don't think me crazy, then?'

'If you are crazy, there have been a great many madmen!' said Agatha.

'Of course there have been a great many. I have said that to myself, and it has helped me. They have gained nothing but the pleasure of their love, and I therefore, in gaining nothing and having nothing, am not worse off than the rest. But they had more than I, didn't they? You see I have had absolutely nothing – not even a glance,' he went on. 'I have never even seen her look at me. I have not only never spoken to her, but I have never been near enough to speak to her. This is all I have ever had – to lay my hand on something she has worn, and yet for the past month I have thought of her night and day. Sitting over there, a hundred rods away, simply because she was sitting in this place, in the same sunshine, looking out on the same sea: that was happiness enough for me. I am dying, but for the last five weeks that has kept me alive. It was for that I got up every day and came out here; but for that, I should have stayed at home and never have got up again. I have never sought to be presented to her, because I didn't wish to trouble her for nothing. It seemed to me it would be an impertinence to tell her of my admiration. I have nothing to offer her – I am but the shadow of a living man, and if I were to say to her, "Madam, I love you," she could only answer, "Well, sir, what then?" Nothing – nothing! To speak to her of what I felt seemed only to open the lid of a grave in her face. It was more delicate not to do that; so I kept my distance and said nothing. Even this, as I say, has been a happiness, but it has been a happiness that has tired me out. This is the last of it. I must give up and make an end!' And he stopped, panting a little, and apparently exhausted with his eloquence.

Agatha had always heard of love at first sight; she had read of it in poems and romances, but she had never been so near to it as this. It seemed to her wonderfully beautiful, and she believed in it devoutly. It made Mr Longstaff brilliantly interesting; it cast a glory over the details of his face and person, and the pleading inflections of his voice. The little English ladies had been right; he was certainly a perfect gentleman. She could trust him.

'Perhaps if you stay at home a while you will get better,' she said, soothingly.

Her tone seemed to him such an indication that she accepted the propriety and naturalness of his passion that he put out his hand, and for an instant laid it on her own.

'I knew you were reasonable – I knew I could talk to you. But I shall not get well. All the great doctors say so, and I believe them. If the passionate desire to get well for a particular purpose could work a miracle and cure a mortal disease, I should have seen the miracle two months ago. To get well and have a right to speak to your friend – that was my passionate desire. But I am worse than ever; I am very weak, and I shall not be able to come out any more. It seemed to me today that I should never see you again, and yet I wanted so much to be able to tell you this! It made me very unhappy. What a wonderful chance it is that she went away! I must be grateful; if Heaven doesn't grant my great prayers it grants my small ones. I beg you to render me this service. Tell her what I have told you. Not now – not till I am gone. Don't trouble her with it while I am in life. Please promise me that. But when I am dead it will seem less importunate, because then you can speak of me in the past. It will be like a story. My servant will come and tell you. Then please say to her – "You were his last thought, and it was his last wish that you should know it." ' He slowly got up and put out his hand; his servant, who had been standing at a distance, came forward with obsequious solemnity as if it were part of his duty to adapt his deportment to the tone of his master's conversation. Agatha Josling took the young man's hand, and he stood and looked at her a moment longer. She too had risen to her feet; she was much impressed.

'You won't tell her until *after* – ?' he said pleadingly. She shook her head. 'And then you will tell her faithfully?' She nodded, he pressed her hand, and then, having raised his hat, he took his servant's arm, and slowly moved away

Agatha kept her word; she said nothing to Diana about her interview. The young Americans came out and sat upon the shore the next day, and the next, and the next, and Agatha watched intently for Mr Longstaff's reappearance. But she watched in vain; day after day he was absent, and his absence confirmed his sad prediction She thought all this a wonderful thing to happen to a woman, and as she glanced askance at her beautiful companion, she was almost irritated at seeing her sit there so careless and serene, while a poor young man was dying, as one might say, of love for her. At moments she wondered whether, in spite of her promise, it were not her Christian duty to tell Diana his story, and give her the chance to go to him. But it occurred to Agatha, who knew very well that her companion had a certain stately pride in which she herself was deficient that even if she were told of his condition Diana might decline to do anything; and this she felt to be a very painful thing to see. Besides, she had promised, and she always kept her promises. But her thoughts were constantly with Mr Longstaff and the romance of the affair. This made her melancholy, and she talked much less than usual. Suddenly she was aroused from a reverie by hearing Diana express a careless curiosity as to what had become of the solitary young man who used to sit on the neighbouring bench and do them the honour to stare at them.

For almost the first time in her life Agatha Josling deliberately dissembled.

'He has either gone away, or he has taken to his bed. I am sure he is dying, alone, in some wretched mercenary lodging.'

'I prefer to believe something more cheerful,' said Diana. 'I believe he is gone to Paris and is eating a beautiful dinner at a great restaurant.

Agatha for a moment said nothing, and then –

'I don't think you care what becomes of him,' she ventured to observe.

'My dear child, why should I care?' Diana demanded.

And Agatha Josling was forced to admit that there really was no particular reason. But the event contradicted her. Three days afterwards she took a long drive with her friend, from which they returned only as dusk was closing in. As they descended from the carriage at the door of their lodging she observed a figure standing in the street, slightly apart, which even in the early darkness had an air of familiarity. A second glance assured her that Mr Longstaff's servant was hovering there in the hope of catching her attention. She immediately determined to give him a liberal measure of it. Diana left the vehicle and passed into the house, while the coachman fortunately asked for orders for the morrow. Agatha briefly gave such as were necessary, and then, before going in, turned to the hovering figure. It approached on tiptoe, hat in hand, and shaking its head very sadly. The old man wore an air of animated affliction which indicated that Mr Longstaff was a generous master, and he proceeded to address Miss Josling in that macaronic French which is usually at the command of Italian domestics who have seen the world.

'I stole away from my dear gentleman's bedside on purpose to have ten words with you. The old woman at the fruit-stall opposite told me that you had gone to drive, so I waited; but it seemed to me a thousand years till you returned!'

'But you have not left your master alone?' said Agatha.

'He has two Sisters of Charity – heaven reward them! They watch with him night and day. He is very low, *pauvre cher homme!*' And the old man looked at the little lady with that clear, human, sympathetic glance, with which Italians of all classes bridge over the social gulf. Agatha felt that he knew his master's secret, and that she might discuss it with him freely.

'Is he dying?' she asked.

'That's the question, dear lady! He is very low. The doctors have given him up; but the doctors don't know his malady. They have felt his dear body all over, they have sounded his lungs, and looked at his tongue and counted his pulse; they know what he eats and drinks – it's soon told! But they haven't seen his *mind* dear lady. I have; and so far I am a better doctor than they. I know his secret – I know that he loves the beautiful girl above!' and the old man pointed to the upper windows of the house.

'Has your master taken you into his confidence?' Agatha demanded.

He hesitated a moment; then shaking his head a little and laying his hand on his heart –

'Ah, dear lady,' he said, 'the point is whether I have taken him into mine. I have not, I confess; he is too far gone. But I have determined to be his doctor and to try a remedy the others have never thought of. Will you help me?'

'If I can,' said Agatha. 'What is your remedy?'

The old man pointed to the upper windows of the house again.

'Your lovely friend! Bring her to his bedside.'

'If he is dying,' said Agatha, 'how would that help him?'

'He is dying for want of it. That's my idea at least, and I think it's worth trying. If a young man loves a beautiful woman, and having never so much as touched the tip of her glove, falls into a mortal illness and wastes away, it requires no great wit to see that his illness doesn't come from his having indulged himself too grossly. It comes rather from the opposite cause! If he sinks when she's away, perhaps he will come up when she's there. At any rate, that's my theory; and any theory is good that will save a dying man. Let the young lady come and stand a moment by his bed, and lay her hand upon his. We shall see what happens. If he gets well it's worth while; if he doesn't, there is no harm done. A young lady risks nothing in going to see a poor gentleman who lies in a stupor between two holy women.'

Agatha was much impressed with this picturesque reasoning, but she answered that it was quite impossible that her beautiful friend should go upon this pious errand without a special invitation from Mr Longstaff. Even should he beg Diana to come to him, Agatha was by no means sure her companion would go; but it was very certain she would not take such an extraordinary step at the mere suggestion of a servant.

'But you, dear lady, have the happiness not to be a servant,' the old man rejoined. 'Let the suggestion be yours.'

'From me it could come with no force, for what am I supposed to know about your poor master?'

'You have not told your friend what my dear master told you the other day?'

Agatha answered this question by another question.

'Did he tell you what he had told me?'

The old man tapped his forehead an instant and smiled.

'A good servant, you know, dear lady, needs never to be told things! If you have not repeated my master's words to the signorina, I beg you very earnestly to do so. I am afraid she is rather cold.'

Agatha glanced a moment at the upper windows, and then she gave a silent nod. She wondered greatly to find herself discussing Diana's character with this aged menial; but the situation was so strange and romantic that one's old landmarks of propriety were quite obliterated, and it seemed natural that an Italian *valet de chambre* should be as frank and familiar as a servant in an old-fashioned comedy.

'If it is necessary that my dear master shall send for the young lady,' Mr Longstaff's domestic resumed, 'I think I can promise you that he will. Let me urge you, meanwhile, to talk to her. If she is cold, warm her up! Prepare her to find him very interesting. If you could see him, poor gentleman, lying there as still and handsome as if he were his own monument in a *campo santo*, I think he would interest you.'

This seemed to Agatha a very touching image, but it occurred to her that her interview with Mr Longstaff's representative, now unduly prolonged, was assuming a nocturnal character. She abruptly brought it to a close, after having assured her interlocutor that she would reflect upon what he had told her; and she rejoined her companion in the deepest agitation. Late that evening her agitation broke out. She went into Diana's room where she found this young lady standing white-robed before her mirror, with her auburn tresses rippling down to her knees; and then, taking her two hands, she told the story of the young Englishman's passion, told of his coming to talk to her that day that Diana had left her alone on the bench by the sea, and of his venerable valet having, a couple of hours before, sought speech of her on the same subject. Diana listened, at first with a rosy flush, and then with a cold, an almost cruel, frown.

'Take pity upon him,' said Agatha Josling – 'take pity upon him, and go and see him.'

'I don't understand,' said her companion, 'and it seems to me very disagreeable. What is Mr Longstaff to me?' But before they separated Agatha had persuaded her to say that, if a message really should come from the young man's death-bed, she would not refuse him the light of her presence.

The message really came, brought of course by the invalid's zealous chamberlain. He reappeared on the morrow, announcing that his master humbly begged for the honour of ten minutes' conversation with the two ladies. They consented to follow him, and he led the way to Mr Longstaff's apartments. Diana still wore her irritated brow, but it made her look more than ever like the easily-startled goddess of the chase. Under the old man's guidance they passed through a low green door in a yellow wall, across a tangled garden full of orange trees and winter roses, and into a white-wainscoted saloon, where they were presently left alone before a great classic Empire clock, perched upon a frigid southern chimney-place. They waited, however, but a few moments; the door of an adjoining room opened, and the Sisters of Charity, in white-winged hoods and with their hands thrust into the loose sleeves of the opposite arm, came forth and stood with downcast eyes on either side of the threshold. Then the old servant appeared between them, and beckoned to the two young girls to advance. The latter complied with a certain hesitation, and he led them into the chamber of the dying man. Here, pointing to the bed, he silently left them and withdrew; not closing, however, the door of communication of the saloon, where he took up his station with the Sisters of Charity.

Diana and her companion stood together in the middle of the darker room, waiting for an invitation to approach their summoner. He lay in his bed, propped up on pillows, with his arms outside the counterpane. For a moment he simply gazed at them; he was as white as the sheet that covered him, and he certainly looked like a dying man. But he had the strength to bend forward, and to speak in a soft distinct voice.

'Would you be so kind as to come nearer?' said Mr Longstaff.

Agatha Josling gently pushed her friend forward, but she followed her to the bedside. Diana stood there, her frown had melted away; and the young man sank back upon his pillows and looked at her. A faint colour came into his face, and he clasped his two hands together on his breast. For some moments he simply gazed at the beautiful girl before him. It was an awkward situation for her, and Agatha expected her at any moment to turn away in disgust. But, slowly, her look of proud compulsion, of mechanical compliance, was exchanged for something more patient and pitying. The young Englishman's face expressed a kind of spiritual ecstasy which, it was impossible not to feel, gave a peculiar sanctity to the occasion.

'It was very generous of you to come,' he said at last. 'I hardly ventured to hope you would. I suppose you know – I suppose your friend, who listened to me so kindly, has told you?'

'Yes, she knows,' murmured Agatha – 'she knows.'

'I did not intend you should know until after my death,' he went on; 'but' – and he paused a moment and shook his clasped hands together – 'I couldn't wait! And when I felt that I couldn't wait, a new idea, a new desire, came into my mind.' He was silent again for an instant, still looking with worshipful entreaty at Diana. The colour in his face deepened. 'It is something that you may do for me. You will think it a most extraordinary request; but in my position a man grows bold. Dear lady, will you marry me?'

'Oh dear!' cried Agatha Josling, just audibly. Her companion said nothing – her attitude seemed to say that in this remarkable situation one thing was no more surprising than another. But she paid Mr Longstaff's proposal the respect of slowly seating herself in a chair which had been placed near his bed; here she rested in maidenly majesty, with her eyes fixed on the ground.

'It will help me to die happy, since die I must!' the young man continued. 'It will enable me to do something for you – the only thing I can do. I have property – lands, houses, a great many beautiful things – things I have loved and am very sorry to be leaving behind me. Lying here helpless and hopeless through so many days, the thought has come to me of what a bliss it would be to know that they should rest in your hands. If you were my wife, they would rest there safely. You might be spared much annoyance; and it is not only that. It is a fancy I have beyond that. It would be the feeling of it! I am fond of life. I don't want to die; but since I must die, it would be a happiness to have got just this out of life – this joining of our hands before a priest. You could go away then. For you it would make no change – it would be no burden. But I should have a few hours in which to lie and think of my happiness.'

There was something in the young man's tone so simple and sincere, so tender and urgent, that Agatha Josling was touched to tears. She turned away to hide them, and went on tiptoe to the window, where she silently let them flow. Diana apparently was not unmoved. She raised her eyes and let them rest kindly on those of Mr Longstaff, who continued softly to urge his proposal. 'It would be a great charity,' he said, 'a great condescension, and it can produce no consequence to you that you could regret. It can only give you a larger liberty. You know very little about me, but I have a feeling that, so far as belief goes, you can believe me, and that is all I ask of you. I don't ask you to love me – that takes time. It is something I can't pretend to. It is only to consent to the form, the ceremony. I have seen the English clergyman, he says he will perform it. He will tell you, besides, all about me – that I am an English gentleman, and that the name I offer you is one of the best in the world.'

It was strange to hear a dying man lie there and argue his point so reasonably and consistently; but now, apparently, his argument was finished. There was a deep silence, and Agatha thought it would be discreet on her own part to retire. She moved quietly into the adjoining room, where the two Sisters of Charity still stood with their hands in their sleeves, and the old Italian valet was taking snuff with a melancholy gesture, like a baffled diplomatist. Agatha turned her back to these people, and, approaching a window again, stood looking out into the garden upon the orange trees and the winter roses. It seemed to her that she had been listening to the most beautiful, most romantic, and most eloquent of declarations. How could Diana be insensible to it? She earnestly hoped her companion would consent to the solemn and interesting ceremony proposed by Mr Longstaff, and though her delicacy had prompted her to withdraw, it permitted her to listen eagerly to what Diana should say. Then (as she heard nothing) it was eclipsed by the desire to go back and whisper, with a sympathetic kiss, a word of counsel. She glanced round again at the Sisters of Charity, who appeared to have perceived that the moment was a critical one. One of them detached herself, and, as Agatha returned, followed her a few steps into the room. Diana had got up from her chair. She was looking about her uneasily – she grasped at Agatha's hand. Reginald Longstaff lay there with his wasted face and his brilliant eyes, looking at them both. Agatha took her friend's two hands in both her own.

'It is very little to do, dearest,' she murmured, 'and it will make him very happy.'

The young man appeared to have heard her, and he repeated her words in a tone of intense entreaty.

'It is very little to do, dearest!'

Diana looked round at him an instant. Then, for an instant, she covered her face with her two hands. Removing them, but holding them still against her cheeks, she looked at her companion with eyes that Agatha always remembered – eyes through which a thin gleam of mockery flashed from the seriousness of her face.

'Suppose, after all, he should not die?' she murmured.

Longstaff heard it; he gave a long soft moan, and turned away. The Sister immediately approached his bed, on the other side, dropped on her knees and bent over him, while he leaned his head against the great white cape upon which her crucifix was displayed. Diana stood a moment longer, looking at him; then, gathering her shawl together with a great dignity, she slowly walked out of the room. Agatha could do nothing but follow her. The old Italian, holding the door open for them to pass out, made them an exaggerated obeisance.

In the garden Diana paused, with a flush in her cheek, and said –

'If he could die with it, he could die without it!' But beyond the garden gate, in the empty sunny street, she suddenly burst into tears.

Agatha made no reproaches, no comments, but her companion, during the rest of the day, spoke of Mr Longstaff several times with an almost passionate indignation. She pronounced his conduct indelicate, egotistic, impertinent; she declared that the scene had been revolting. Agatha, for the moment, remained silent, but the next day she attempted to make some vague apology for the poor young man. Then Diana, with passionate emphasis, begged her to be so good as never to mention his name again; and she added that this disgusting incident had put her completely out of humour with Nice, from which place they would immediately take their departure. That they did without delay; they began to travel again Agatha heard no more of Reginald Longstaff; the English ladies who had been her original source of information with regard to him had now left Nice; otherwise she would have written to them for news. That is, she would have thought of writing to them; I suspect that, on the whole, she would have denied herself this satisfaction, on the ground of loyalty to her friend. Agatha, at any rate, could only drop a tear, at solitary hours, upon the young man's unanswered prayer and early death. It must be confessed, however, that sometimes, as the weeks elapsed, a certain faint displeasure mingled itself with her sympathy – a wish that, roughly speaking, poor Mr Longstaff had left them alone. Since that strange interview at his bedside things had not gone well, the charm of their earlier wanderings seemed broken. Agatha said to herself that, really, if she were superstitious, she might fancy that Diana's conduct on this occasion had brought them under an evil spell. It was no superstition, certainly, to think that this young lady had lost a certain generous mildness of temper. She was impatient absent-minded, indifferent, capricious. She expressed unaccountable opinions and proposed unnatural plans. It is true that disagreeable things were constantly happening to them – things which would have taxed the most unruffled spirit. Their post-horses broke down, their postilions were impertinent, their luggage went astray, their servants betrayed them. The heavens themselves seemed to join in the conspiracy, and for days together were dark and ungenerous, treating them only to wailing winds and watery clouds. It was, in a large measure, in the light of after years that Agatha judged this period; but even at the time she felt it to be depressing, uncomfortable, unnatural. Diana apparently shared her opinion of it, though she never openly avowed it. She took refuge in a kind of haughty silence, and whenever a new disaster came to her knowledge she simply greeted it with a bitter smile – a smile which Agatha always interpreted as an ironical reflection on poor, fantastic, obtrusive Mr Longstaff, who, through some mysterious action upon the machinery of nature, had turned the tide of their fortunes. At the end of the summer, suddenly, Diana proposed they should go home, speaking of it in the tone of a person who gives up a hopeless struggle. Agatha assented, and the two ladies returned to America, much to the relief of Miss Josling, who had an uncomfortable sense that there was something unexpressed and unregulated between them, which gave their intercourse a resemblance to a sultry morning. But at home they separated very tenderly, for Agatha had to go into the country and devote herself to her nearer kinsfolk. These good people, after her long absence, were exacting, so that for two years she saw nothing of her late companion.

She often, however, heard from her, and Diana figured in the town-talk that was occasionally wafted to her rural home. She sometimes figured strangely – as a rattling coquette who carried on flirtations by the hundred and broke hearts by the dozen. This had not been Diana's former character, and Agatha found matter for meditation in the change. But the young lady's own letters said little of her admirers and displayed no trophies. They came very fitfully – sometimes at the rate of a dozen a month and sometimes not at all; but they were usually of a serious and abstract cast, and contained the author's opinions upon life, death, religion immortality. Mistress of her actions and of a pretty fortune, it might have been expected that news would come in trustworthy form of Diana's having at last accepted one of her rumoured lovers. Such news in fact came, and it was apparently trustworthy, inasmuch as it proceeded from the young lady herself. She wrote to Agatha that she was to be married, and Agatha immediately congratulated her upon her happiness. Then Diana wrote back that though she was to be married she was not at all happy; and she shortly afterwards added that she was neither happy nor to be married. She had broken off her projected union, and her felicity was smaller than ever. Poor Agatha was sorely perplexed, and she found it a comfort that, a month after this, her friend should have sent her a peremptory summons to come to her. She immediately obeyed.

Arriving, after a long journey, at the dwelling of her young hostess, she saw Diana at the farther end of the drawing-room, with her back turned, looking out of the window. She was evidently watching for Agatha but Miss Josling had come in, by accident, through a private entrance which was not visible from the window. She gently approached her friend, and then Diana turned. She had her two hands laid upon her cheeks, and her eyes were sad; her face and attitude suggested something that Agatha had seen before and kept the memory of. While she kissed her, Agatha remembered that it was just so she had stood for that last moment before poor Mr Longstaff.

'Will you come abroad with me again?' Diana asked. 'I am very ill.'

'Dearest, what is the matter?' said Agatha.

'I don't know; I believe I am dying. They tell me this place is bad for me; that I must have another climate; that I must move about. Will you take care of me? I shall be very easy to take care of now.'

Agatha, for all answer, embraced her afresh, and as soon after this as possible the two friends embarked again for Europe. Miss Josling had thrown herself the more freely into this scheme, as her companion's appearance seemed a striking confirmation of her words. Not, indeed, that she looked as if she were dying; but in the two years that had elapsed since their separation she had wasted and faded. She looked more than two years older, and the brilliancy of her beauty was dimmed.

She was pale and languid, and she moved more slowly than when she seemed a goddess treading the forest leaves. The beautiful statue had grown human and taken on some of the imperfections of humanity. And yet the doctors by no means affirmed that she had a mortal malady, and when one of them was asked by an inquisitive matron why he had recommended this young lady to cross the seas, he replied with a smile that it was a principle in his system to prescribe the remedies that his patients greatly desired.

At present the fair travellers had no misadventures. The broken charm had renewed itself; the heavens smiled upon them, and their postilions treated them like princesses. Diana, too, had completely recovered her native serenity; she was the gentlest, the most docile, the most reasonable of women. She was silent and subdued, as was natural in an invalid; though in one important particular her demeanour was certainly at variance with the idea of debility. She had much more taste for motion than for rest, and constant change of place became the law of her days. She wished to see all the places that she had not seen before, and all the old ones over again.

'If I am really dying,' she said, smiling softly, 'I must leave my farewell cards everywhere.' So she passed her days in a great open carriage, leaning back in it and looking, right and left, at everything she passed. On her former journey to Europe she had seen but little of England, and now she determined to visit the whole of this famous island. She rolled for weeks through the beautiful English landscape, past meadows and hedgerows, over the avenues of great estates and under the walls of castles and abbeys. For the English parks and manors, the 'Halls' and 'Courts,' she had an especial admiration, and into the grounds of such as were open to appreciative tourists she made a point of penetrating. Here she stayed her carriage beneath the oaks and beeches, and sat for an hour at a time listening to nightingales and watching browsing deer. She never failed to visit a residence that lay on her road, and as soon as she arrived at a town she inquired punctiliously whether there were any fine country-seats in the neighbourhood. In this delightful fashion she spent a whole summer. Through the autumn she continued to wander restlessly; she visited, on the Continent, a hundred watering-places and travellers' resorts. The beginning of the winter found her in Rome, where she confessed to being very tired and prepared to seek repose.

'I am weary, weary,' she said to her companion. 'I didn't know how weary I was. I feel like sinking down in this City of Rest, and resting here for ever.'

She took a lodging in an old palace, where her chamber was hung with ancient tapestries, and her drawing-room decorated with the arms of a pope. Here, giving way to her fatigue, she ceased to wander. The only thing she did was to go every day to St Peter's. She went nowhere else. She sat at her window all day with a big book in her lap, which she never read looking out into a Roman garden at a fountain plashing into a weedy alcove, and half a dozen nymphs in mottled marble. Sometimes she told her companion that she was happier this way than she had ever been – in this way, and in going to St Peter's. In the great church she often spent the whole afternoon. She had a servant behind her, carrying a stool; he placed her stool against a marble pilaster, and she sat there for a long time, looking up into the airy hollow of the dome and over the vast peopled pavement. She noticed every one who passed her; but Agatha, lingering beside her, felt less at liberty, she hardly knew why, to make remarks about the people around them than she had felt when they sat upon the shore at Nice.

One day Agatha left her and strolled about the church by herself. The ecclesiastical life of Rome had not shrunken to its present smallness, and in one corner or another of St Peter's there was always some occasion of worship. Agatha found plenty of entertainment, and was absent for half an hour. When she came back she found her companion's place deserted, and she sat down on the empty stool to await her reappearance. Some time elapsed, and then she wandered away in quest of her. She found her at last, near one of the side-altars; but she was not alone. A gentleman stood before her whom she appeared just to have encountered. Her face was very pale, and its expression led Agatha to look straightway at the stranger. Then she saw he was no stranger; he was Reginald Longstaff! He, too, evidently had been much startled, but he was already recovering himself. He stood very gravely an instant longer; then he silently bowed to the two ladies and turned away.

Agatha felt at first as if she had seen a ghost; but the impression was immediately corrected by the fact that Mr Longstaff's aspect was very much less ghostly than it had been in life. He looked like a strong man he held himself upright, and had a handsome colour. What Agatha saw in Diana's face was not surprise; it was a pale radiance which she waited a moment to give a name to. Diana put out her hand and laid it in her arm, and her touch helped Agatha to know what it was that her face expressed. Then she felt too that this knowledge itself was not a surprise; she seemed to have been waiting for it. She looked at her friend again, and Diana was beautiful. Diana blushed and became more beautiful yet. Agatha led her back to her seat near the marble pilaster.

'So you were right,' Agatha said presently. 'He would, after all, have got well!'

Diana would not sit down; she motioned to her servant to bring away the stool, and continued to move towards the door. She said nothing until she stood without, in the great square, between the colonnades and fountains. Then she spoke.

'I am right now, but I was wrong, then. He got well because I refused him. I gave him a hurt that cured him.'

That evening, beneath the Roman lamps in the great drawing-room of the arms of the pope, a remarkable conversation took place between the two friends. Diana wept and hid her face; but her tears and her shame were gratuitous. Agatha felt, as I have said, that she had already guessed all the unexplained, and it was needless for her companion to tell her that, three weeks after she had refused Reginald Longstaff, she insanely loved him. It was needless that Diana should confess that his image had never been out of her mind, that she believed he was still among the living, and that she had come back to Europe with a desperate hope of meeting him. It was in this hope that she had wandered from town to town and looked at every one who passed her; and it was in this hope that she had lingered in so many English parks. She knew her love was very strange; she could only say it had consumed her. It had all come upon her afterwards – in retrospect, in meditation. Or rather, she supposed, it had been there always, since she first saw him, and the revulsion from displeasure to pity, after she left his bedside, had brought it out. And with it came the faith that he had indeed got well, both of his malady and of his own passion. This was her punishment! And then she spoke with a divine simplicity which Agatha, weeping a little too, wished that, if this belief of Diana's were true, the young man might have heard. 'I am so glad he is well and strong. And that he looks so handsome and so good!' And she presently added, 'Of course he has got well only to hate me. He wishes never to see me again. Very good. I have had my wish; I have seen him once more. That was what I wanted, and I can die content.'

It seemed in fact as if she were going to die. She went no more to St Peter's, and exposed herself to no more encounters with Mr Longstaff. She sat at her window and looked out at the freckled dryads and the cypresses, or wandered about her quarter of the palace with a vaguely-smiling resignation. Agatha watched her with a sadness that was less submissive. This too was something that she had heard of, that she had read of in poetry and fable, but that she had never supposed she should see – her companion was dying of love! Agatha thought of many things, and made up her mind upon several. The first of these latter was to send for the doctor. This personage came, and Diana let him look at her through his spectacles and hold her white wrist. He announced that she was ill, and she smiled and said she knew it; and then he gave her a little phial of gold-coloured fluid, which he bade her to drink. He recommended her to remain in Rome, as the climate exactly suited her complaint. Agatha's second desire was to see Mr Longstaff, who had appealed to her, she reflected, in the day of his own tribulation, and whom she therefore had a right to approach at present. She found it impossible to believe, too, that the passion which led him to take that extraordinary step at Nice was extinct such passions as that never died. If he had made no further attempt to see Diana, it was because he believed that she was still as cold as when she turned away from his death-bed. It must be added, moreover, that Agatha felt a lawful curiosity to learn how from that death-bed he had risen again into blooming manhood. This last point there was no theory to explain.

Agatha went to St Peter's, feeling sure that sooner or later she should encounter him there. At the end of a week she perceived him, and seeing her, he immediately came and spoke to her. As Diana had said, he was now extremely handsome, and he looked particularly good. He was a quiet, blooming, gallant young English gentleman. He seemed much embarrassed, but his manner to Agatha expressed the highest consideration.

'You must think me a dreadful impostor,' he said, very gravely. 'But I *was* dying – or I believed I was.'

'And by what miracle did you recover?'

He was silent a moment, and then he said –

'I suppose it was by the miracle of wounded pride!' She noticed that he asked nothing about Diana; and presently she felt that he knew she was thinking of this. 'The strangest part of it,' he added, 'was, that when my strength came back to me, what had gone before had become as a simple dream. And what happened to me here the other day,' he went on, 'failed to make it a reality again!'

Agatha looked at him a moment in silence, and saw again that he was handsome and kind; and then dropping a sigh over the wonderful mystery of things, she turned sadly away. That evening Diana said to her –

'I know that you have seen him!'

Agatha came to her and kissed her.

'And I am nothing to him now?'

'My own dearest – ' murmured Agatha.

Diana had drunk the little phial of gold-coloured liquid; but after this she ceased to wander about the palace; she never left her room. The old doctor was with her constantly now, and he continued to say that the air of Rome was very good for her complaint. Agatha watched her in helpless sadness; she saw her fading and sinking, and yet she was unable to comfort her. She tried once to comfort her by saying hard things about Mr Longstaff, by pointing out that he had not been honourable; rising herein to a sublime hypocrisy, for on that last occasion at St Peter's the poor girl had felt that she herself admired him as much as ever – that the timid little flame which was kindled at Nice was beginning to shoot up again. Agatha saw nothing but his good looks and his kind manner.

'What did he want – what did he mean, after all?' she pretended to murmur, leaning over Diana's sofa. 'Why should he have been wounded at what you said? It would have been part of the bargain that he should not get well. Did he mean to take an unfair advantage – to make you his wife under false pretences? When you put your finger on the weak spot, why should he resent it? No, it was not honourable.'

Diana smiled sadly; she had no false shame now, and she spoke of this thing as if it concerned another person.

'He would have counted on my forgiving him!' she said. A little while after this she began to sink more rapidly. Then she called her friend to her, and said simply, 'Send for him!' And as Agatha looked perplexed and distressed, she added, 'I know he is still in Rome.'

Agatha at first was at a loss where to find him, but among the benefits of the papal dispensation was the fact that the pontifical police could instantly help you to lay your hand upon any sojourner in the Eternal City. Mr Longstaff had a passport in detention by the government, and this document formed a basis of instruction to the servant whom Agatha sent to interrogate the authorities. The servant came back with the news that he had seen the distinguished stranger, who would wait upon the ladies at the hour they proposed. When this hour came and Mr Longstaff was announced, Diana said to her companion that she must remain with her. It was an afternoon in spring; the high windows into the ancient garden were open, and the room was adorned with great sheaves and stacks of the abundant Roman flowers. Diana sat in a deep arm-chair.

It was certainly a difficult position for Reginald Longstaff. He stopped on the threshold and looked a while at the woman to whom he had made his extraordinary offer; then, pale and agitated, he advanced rapidly towards her. He was evidently shocked at the state in which he found her; he took her hand, and, bending over it, raised it to his lips. She fixed her eyes on him a little, and she smiled a little.

'It is I who am dying now,' she said. 'And now I want to ask something of *you* – to ask what you asked of me.'

He stared, and a deep flush of colour came into his face; he hesitated for an appreciable moment. Then lowering his head with a movement of assent, he kissed her hand again.

'Come back tomorrow,' she said; 'that is all I ask of you.'

He looked at her again for a while in silence; then he abruptly turned and left her. She sent for the English clergyman and told him that she was a dying woman, and that she wished the marriage service to be read beside her couch. The clergyman, too, looked at her in much surprise; but he consented to humour so tenderly romantic a whim, and made an appointment for the afternoon of the morrow. Diana was very tranquil. She sat motionless, with her hands clasped and her eyes closed. Agatha wandered about, arranging and rearranging the flowers. On the morrow she encountered Mr Longstaff in one of the outer rooms: he had come before his time. She made this objection to his being admitted; but he answered that he knew he was early, and had come with intention; he wished to spend the intervening hour with his prospective bride. So he went in and sat down by her couch again, and Agatha, leaving them alone, never knew what passed between them. At the end of the hour the clergyman arrived, and read the marriage service to them, pronouncing the nuptial blessing, while Agatha stood by as witness. Mr Longstaff went through all this with a solemn, inscrutable face, and Agatha, observing him, said to herself that one must at least do him the justice to admit that he was performing punctiliously what honour demanded. When the clergyman had gone he asked Diana when he might see her again.

'Never!' she said, with her strange smile. And she added – 'I shall not live long now.'

He kissed her face, but he was obliged to leave her. He gave Agatha an anxious look, as if he wished to say something to her, but she preferred not to listen to him. After this Diana sank rapidly. The next day Reginald Longstaff came back and insisted upon seeing Agatha.

'Why should she die?' he asked. 'I want her to live.'

'Have you forgiven her?' said Agatha.

'She saved me!' he cried.

Diana consented to see him once more; there were two doctors in attendance now, and they also had consented. He knelt down beside her bed and asked her to live. But she feebly shook her head.

'It would be wrong of me,' she said.

Later, when he came back once more, Agatha told him she was gone. He stood wondering, with tears in his eyes.

'I don't understand,' he said. 'Did she love me or not?'

'She loved you,' said Agatha, 'more than she believed you could now love her; and it seemed to her that, when she had had her moment of happiness, to leave you at liberty was the tenderest way she could show it!'

BENVOLIO

Chapter 1

ONCE UPON A TIME (as if he had lived in a fairy tale) there was a very interesting young man. This is not a fairy tale, and yet our young man was in some respects as pretty a fellow as any fairy prince. I call him interesting because his type of character is one I have always found it profitable to observe. If you fail to consider him so, I shall be willing to confess that the fault is mine and not his; I shall have told my story with too little skill.

His name was Benvolio; that is, it was not: but we shall call him so for the sake both of convenience and of picturesqueness. He was about to enter upon the third decade of our mortal span; he had a little property, and he followed no regular profession. His personal appearance was in the highest degree prepossessing. Having said this, it were perhaps well that I should let you – you especially, madam – suppose that he exactly corresponded to your ideal of manly beauty; but I am bound to explain definitely wherein it was that he resembled a fairy prince, and I need furthermore to make a record of certain little peculiarities and anomalies in which it is probable that your brilliant conception would be deficient. Benvolio was slim and fair, with clustering locks, remarkably fine eyes, and such a frank, expressive smile, that on the journey through life it was almost as serviceable to its owner as the magic key, or the enchanted ring, or the wishing-cap, or any other bauble of necromantic properties. Unfortunately this charming smile was not always at his command, and its place was sometimes occupied by a very perverse and dusky frown, which rendered the young man no service whatever – not even that of frightening people; for though it expressed extreme irritation and impatience, it was characterised by the brevity of contempt, and the only revenge upon disagreeable things and offensive people that it seemed to express a desire for on Benvolio's part, was that of forgetting and ignoring them with the utmost possible celerity. It never made any one tremble, though now and then it perhaps made irritable people murmur an imprecation or two. You might have supposed from Benvolio's manner, when he was in good humour (which was the greater part of the time), from his brilliant, intelligent glance, from his easy, irresponsible step, and in especial from the sweet, clear, lingering, caressing tone of his voice – the voice, as it were, of a man whose fortune has been made for him, and who assumes, a trifle egotistically, that the rest of the world is equally at leisure to share with him the sweets of life, to pluck the wayside flowers, and chase the butterflies afield – you might have supposed, I say, from all this luxurious assurance of demeanour, that our hero really had the wishing-cap sitting invisible on his handsome brow, or was obliged only to close his knuckles together a moment to exert an effective pressure upon the magic ring. The young man, I have said, was a mixture of inconsistencies; I may say more exactly that he was a tissue of contradictions. He did possess the magic ring, in a certain fashion; he possessed, in other words, the poetic imagination. Everything that fancy could do for him was done in perfection. It gave him immense satisfactions; it transfigured the world; it made very common objects sometimes seem radiantly beautiful, and it converted beautiful ones into infinite sources of intoxication. Benvolio had what is called the poetic temperament. It is rather out of fashion to describe a man in these terms; but I believe, in spite of much evidence to the contrary, that there are poets still; and if we may call a spade a spade, why should we not call such a person as Benvolio a poet?

These contradictions that I speak of ran through his whole nature, and they were perfectly apparent in his habits, in his manners, in his conversation, and even in his physiognomy. It was as if the souls of two very different men had been placed together to make the voyage of life in the same boat, and had agreed for convenience' sake to take the helm in alternation. The helm, with Benvolio, was always the imagination; but in his different moods it worked very differently. To an acute observer his face itself would have betrayed these variations; and it is certain that his dress, his talk, his way of spending his time, one day and another, abundantly indicated them. Sometimes he looked very young – rosy, radiant, blooming, younger than his years. Then suddenly, as the light struck his head in a particular manner, you would see that his golden locks contained a surprising number of silver threads; and with your attention quickened by this discovery, you would proceed to detect something grave and discreet in his smile – something vague and ghostly, like the dim adumbration of the darker half of the lunar disk. You might have met Benvolio, in certain states of mind, dressed like a man of the highest fashion, wearing his hat on his ear, a rose in his button-hole, a wonderful intaglio or an antique Syracusan coin, by way of a pin, in his cravat. Then, on the morrow, you would have espied him braving the sunshine in a rusty scholar's coat, with his hat pulled over his brow – a costume wholly at odds with flowers and gems. It was all a matter of fancy; but his fancy was a weathercock, and faced east or west as the wind blew. His conversation matched his coat and breeches; he talked one day the talk of the town; he chattered, he gossiped, he asked questions and told stories; you would have said that he was a charming fellow for a dinner-party or the pauses of a cotillon. The next he either talked philosophy or politics, or said nothing at all; he was absent and indifferent; he was thinking his own thoughts: he had a book in his pocket, and evidently he was composing one in his head. At home he lived in two chambers. One was an immense room, hung with pictures, lined with books, draped with rugs and tapestries, decorated with a multitude of ingenious devices (for of all these things he was very fond); the other, his sleeping-room, was almost as bare as a monastic cell. It had a meagre little strip of carpet on the floor, and a dozen well-thumbed volumes of classic poets and sages on the mantel-shelf. On the wall hung three or four coarsely-engraved portraits of the most exemplary of these worthies; these were the only ornaments. But the room had the charm of a great window, in a deep embrasure, looking out upon a tangled, silent, moss-grown garden, and in the embrasure stood the little ink-blotted table at which Benvolio did most of his poetic scribbling. The windows of his sumptuous sitting-room commanded a wide public square, where people were always passing and lounging, where military music used to play on vernal nights, and half the life of the great town went forward. At the risk of your thinking our hero a sad idler, I will say that he spent an inordinate amount of time in gazing out of these windows (in either direction) with his elbows on the sill. The garden did not belong to the house which he inhabited, but to a neighbouring one, and the proprietor, a graceless old miser, was very chary of permits to visit his domain. But Benvolio's fancy used to wander through the alleys without stirring the long arms of the untended plants, and to bend over the heavy-headed flowers without leaving a footprint on their beds. It was here that his happiest thoughts came to him – that inspiration (as we may say, speaking of a man of the poetic temperament) descended upon him in silence, and for certain divine, appreciable moments, stood poised along the course of his scratching quill. It was not, however, that he had not spent some very charming hours in the larger, richer apartment. He used to receive his friends there – sometimes in great numbers, sometimes at boister-ous, many-voiced suppers, which lasted far into the night. When these entertainments were over he never made a direct transition to his little scholar's cell. He went out and wandered for an hour through the dark sleeping streets of the town, ridding himself of the fumes of wine, and feeling not at all tipsy, but intensely, portentously sober. More than once, when he had come back and prepared to go to bed, he saw the first faint glow of dawn trembling upward over the tree-tops of his garden. His friends, coming to see him, often found the greater room empty, and advancing, rapped at the door of his chamber. But he subsequently kept quiet, not desiring in the least to see them knowing exactly what they were going to say, and not thinking it worth hearing. Then, hearing them slide away, and the outer door close behind them, he would come forth and take a turn in his slippers, over his Persian carpets, and glance out of the window and see his defeated visitant stand scratching his chin in the sunny square. After this he would laugh lightly to himself – as is said to be the habit of the scribbling tribe in moments of production.

Although he had many relatives he enjoyed extreme liberty. His family was so large, his brothers and sisters were so numerous, that he could absent himself and be little missed. Sometimes he used this privilege freely; he tired of people whom he had seen very often, and he had seen, of course, a great deal of his family. At other moments he was extremely domestic, he suddenly found solitude depressing, and it seemed to him that if one sought society as a refuge, one needed to be on familiar terms with it, and that with no one was familiarity so natural as among people who had grown up at a common fireside. Nevertheless it frequently occurred to him – for sooner or later everything occurred to him – that he was too independent and irresponsible, that he would be happier if he had a little golden ball and chain tied to his ankle. His curiosity about all things – life and love and art and truth – was great, and his theory was to satisfy it as freely as might be; but as the years went by this pursuit of impartial science appeared to produce a singular result. He became conscious of an intellectual condition similar to that of a palate which has lost its relish. To a man with a disordered appetite all things taste alike, and so it seemed to Benvolio that the gustatory faculty of his mind was losing its keenness. It had still its savoury moments, its feasts and its holidays; but, on the whole, the spectacle of human life was growing flat and stale. This is simply a wordy way of expressing that comprehensive fact – Benvolio was *blasé*. He knew it, he knew it betimes, and he regretted it acutely. He believed that the mind can keep its freshness to the last, and that it is only fools that are overbored. There was a way of never being bored, and the wise man's duty was to find it out. One of its rudiments, he believed was that one grows tired of one's self sooner than of anything else in the world. Idleness, every one admitted, was the greatest of follies; but idleness was subtle, and exacted tribute under a hundred plausible disguises. One was often idle when one seemed to be ardently occupied; one was always idle when one's occupation had not a high aim. One was idle, therefore, when one was working simply for one's self. Curiosity for curiosity's sake, art for art's sake, these were essentially broken-winded steeds. Ennui was at the end of everything that did not multiply our relations with life. To multiply his relations, therefore, Benvolio reflected, should be the wise man's aim. Poor Benvolio had to reflect on this, because, as I say, he was a poet and not a man of action. A fine fellow of the latter stamp would have solved the problem without knowing it, and bequeathed to his fellow men not frigid formulas but vivid examples. But Benvolio had often said to himself that he was born to imagine great things – not to do them; and he had said this by no means sadly, for, on the whole, he was very well content with his portion. Imagine them he determined he would, and on a magnificent scale. He would multiply his labours, at least, and they should be very serious ones. He would cultivate great ideas, he would enunciate great truths, he would write immortal verses. In all this there was a large amount of talent and a liberal share of ambition. I *will* not say that Benvolio was a man of genius; it may seem to make the distinction too cheap; but he was at any rate a man with an intellectual passion; and if, being near him, you had been able to listen intently enough, he would, like the great people of his craft, have seemed to emit something of that vague magical murmur – the voice of the infinite – which lurks in the involutions of a sea-shell. He himself, by the way, had once made use of this little simile, and had written a poem in which it was melodiously set forth that the poetic minds scattered about the world correspond to the little shells one picks up on the beach, all resonant with the echo of ocean. The whole thing was of course rounded off with the sands of time, the waves of history, and other harmonious conceits.

Chapter 2

But (as you are naturally expecting to hear) Benvolio knew perfectly well that there is one relation with life which is a better antidote to ennui than any other – the relation established with a charming woman. Benvolio was of course in love. Who was his mistress, you ask (I flatter myself with some impatience), and was she pretty, was she kind, was he successful? Hereby hangs my tale, which I must relate in due form.

Benvolio's mistress was a lady whom (as I cannot tell you her real name) it will be quite in keeping to speak of as the Countess. The Countess was a young widow, who had some time since divested herself of her mourning weeds – which indeed she had never worn but very lightly. She was rich, extremely pretty, and free to do as she listed. She was passionately fond of pleasure and admiration, and they gushed forth at her feet in unceasing streams. Her beauty was not of the conventional type, but it was dazzlingly brilliant; few faces were more expressive, more fascinating. Hers was never the same for two days together; it reflected her momentary circumstances with extraordinary vividness, and in knowing her you had the advantage of knowing a dozen different women. She was clever and accomplished, and had the credit of being perfectly amiable, indeed, it was difficult to imagine a person combining a greater number of the precious gifts of nature and fortune. She represented felicity, gaiety, success; she was made to charm, to play a part, to exert a sway. She lived in a great house, behind high verdure-muffled walls, where other Countesses, in other years, had played a part no less brilliant. It was an antiquated quarter, into which the tide of commerce had lately begun to roll heavily; but the turbid wave of trade broke in vain against the Countess's enclosure, and if in her garden and her drawing-room you heard the deep uproar of the city, it was only as a vague undertone to sweeter things – to music, and witty talk and tender colloquy. There was something very striking in this little oasis of luxury and privacy in the midst of common toil and traffic.

Benvolio was a great deal at this lady's house; he rarely desired better entertainment. I spoke just now of privacy; but privacy was not what he found there, nor what he wished to find. He went there when he wished to learn with the least trouble what was going on in the world; for the talk of the people the Countess generally had about her was an epitome of the gossip, the rumours, the interests, the hopes and fears, of polite society. She was a thoroughly liberal hostess; all she asked was to be entertained; if you would contribute to the common fund of amusement, of discussion, you were a welcome guest. Sooner or later, among your fellow-guests, you encountered every one of consequence. There were frivolous people and wise people; people whose fortune was in their pockets, and people whose fortune was in their brains; people deeply concerned in public affairs, and people concerned only with the fit of their garments or with the effect upon the company of the announcement of their names. Benvolio, with his taste for a large and various social spectacle, appreciated all this; but he was best pleased, as a general thing, when he found the Countess alone. This was often his fortune, for the simple reason that when the Countess expected him she invariably caused herself to be refused to every one else. This is almost an answer to your inquiry whether Benvolio was successful in his suit. As yet, strictly speaking, there was no suit; Benvolio had never made love to the Countess. This sounds very strange, but it is nevertheless true. He was in love with her; he thought her the most charming creature conceivable; he spent hours with her alone by her own orders; he had had opportunity – he had been up to his neck in opportunity – and yet he had never said to her, as would have seemed so natural, 'Dear Countess, I beseech you to be my wife.' If you are surprised, I may also confide to you that the Countess was; and surprise under the circumstances very easily became displeasure. It is by no means certain that if Benvolio had made the little speech we have just imagined the Countess would have fallen into his arms, confessed to an answering flame, and rung in *finis* to our tale with the wedding-bells. But she nevertheless expected him in civility to pay her this supreme compliment. Her answer would be – what it might be; but his silence was a permanent offence. Every man, roughly speaking, had asked the Countess to marry him, and every man had been told that she was much obliged, but had not been thinking of changing her condition. But here, with the one man who failed to ask her, she was perpetually thinking of it, and this negative quality in Benvolio was more present to her mind, gave her more to think about, than all the positiveness of her other suitors. The truth was, she liked Benvolio extremely, and his independence rendered him excellent service. The Countess had a very lively fancy, and she had fingered, nimbly enough, the volume of the young man's merits. She was by nature a trifle cold; she rarely lost her head; she measured each step as she took it; she had had little fancies and incipient passions; but, on the whole, she had thought much more about love than felt it. She had often tried to form an image of the sort of man it would be well for her to love – for so it was she expressed it. She had succeeded but indifferently, and her imagination had never found a pair of wings until the day she met Benvolio. Then it seemed to her that her quest was ended – her prize gained. This nervous, ardent, deep-eyed youth struck her as the harmonious counterpart of her own facile personality. This conviction rested with the Countess on a fine sense of propriety which it would be vain to attempt to analyse; he was different from herself and from the other men who surrounded her, and she valued him as a specimen of a rare and distinguished type. In the old days she would have appointed him to be her minstrel or her jester – it is to be feared that poor Benvolio would have figured rather dismally in the latter capacity; and at present a woman who was in her own right a considerable social figure, might give such a man a place in her train as an illustrious husband. I don't know how good a judge the Countess was of such matters, but she believed that the world would hear of Benvolio. She had beauty, ancestry, money, luxury, but she had not genius; and if genius was to be had, why not secure it, and complete the list? This is doubtless a rather coarse statement of the Countess's argument, but you have it thrown in gratis as it were; for all I am bound to tell you is that this charming young woman took a fancy to this clever young man, and that she used to cry sometimes for a quarter of a minute when she imagined he was indifferent to her. Her tears were wasted, because he really cared for her – more even than she would have imagined if she had taken a favourable view of the case. But Benvolio, I cannot too much repeat, was an exceedingly complex character, and there was many a lapse in the logic of his conduct. The Countess charmed him, excited him, interested him; he did her abundant justice – more than justice, but at the end of all he felt that she failed to satisfy him. If a man could have half a dozen wives – and Benvolio had once maintained, poetically, that he ought to have – the Countess would do very well for one of them – possibly even for the best of them. But she would not serve for all seasons and all moods; she needed a complement, an alternative – what the French call a *repoussoir*. One day he was going to see her, knowing that he was expected. There was to be a number of other people – in fact, a very brilliant assembly, but Benvolio knew that a certain touch of the hand, a certain glance of the eye, a certain caress of the voice, would be reserved for him alone. Happy Benvolio, you will say, to be going about the world with such charming secrets as this locked up in his young heart! Happy Benvolio indeed; but mark how he trifled with his happiness. He went to the Countess's gate, but he went no farther; he stopped, stood there a moment, frowning intensely, and biting the finger of his glove; then suddenly he turned and strode away in the opposite direction. He walked and walked, and left the town behind him. He went his way till he reached the country, and here he bent his steps toward a little wood which he knew very well, and whither indeed, on a spring afternoon, when she had taken a fancy to play at shepherd and shepherdess, he had once come with the Countess. He flung himself on the grass, on the edge of the wood – not in the same place where he had lain at the Countess's feet, pulling sonnets out of his pocket and reading them one by one; a little stream flowed beside him; opposite, the sun was declining; the distant city lay before him, lifting its towers and chimneys against the reddening western sky. The twilight fell and deepened, and the stars came out. Benvolio lay there thinking that he preferred them to the Countess's wax candles. He went back to town in a farmer's waggon, talking with the honest rustic who drove it.

Very much in this way, when he had been on the point of knocking at the gate of the Countess's heart and asking ardently to be admitted, he had paused, stood frowning, and then turned short and rambled away into solitude. She never knew how near, two or three times, he had come. Two or three times she had accused him of being rude, and this was nothing but the backward swing of the pendulum. One day it seemed to her that he was altogether too vexatious, and she reproached herself with her good nature. She had made herself too cheap; such conduct was beneath her dignity; she would take another tone. She closed her door to him, and bade her people say, whenever he came, that she was engaged. At first Benvolio only wondered. Oddly enough, he was not what is commonly called sensitive; he never supposed you meant to offend him; not being at all impertinent himself, he was not on the watch for impertinence in others. Only when he fairly caught you in the act, he was immensely disgusted. Therefore, as I say, he simply wondered what had suddenly made the Countess so busy; then he remembered certain other charming persons whom he knew, and went to see how the world wagged with them. But they rendered the Countess eminent service she gained by comparison, and Benvolio began to miss her. All that other charming women were who led the life of the world (as it is called) the Countess was in a superior, in a perfect degree; she was the ripest fruit of a high civilisation; her companions and rivals, beside her, had but a pallid bloom, an acrid savour. Benvolio had a relish in all things for the best, and he found himself breathing sighs under the Countess's darkened windows. He wrote to her, asking why in the world she treated him so cruelly, and then she knew that her charm was working. She was careful not to answer his letter, and to see that he was refused at her gate as inexorably as ever. It is an ill wind that blows nobody good, and Benvolio, one night after his dismissal, wandered about the moonlit streets till nearly morning, composing the finest verses he had ever produced. The subscribers to the magazine to which he sent them were at least the gainers. But unlike many poets, Benvolio did not on this occasion bury his passion in his poem; or if he did, its ghost was stalking abroad the very next night. He went again to the Countess's gate, and again it was closed in his face. So, after a very moderate amount of hesitation, he bravely (and with a dexterity which surprised him) scaled her garden wall and dropped down in the moonshine upon her lawn. I don't know whether she was expecting him, but if she had been, the matter could not have been better arranged. She was sitting in a little niche of shrubbery, with no protector but a microscopic lap-dog. She pretended to be scandalised at his audacity, but his audacity carried the hour. 'This time certainly,' thought the Countess, 'he will make his declaration. He didn't jump that wall, at the risk of his neck, simply to ask me for a cup of tea.' Not a bit of it; Benvolio was devoted, but he was not more explicit than before. He declared that this was the happiest hour of his life; that there was a charming air of romance in his position; that honestly, he thanked the Countess for having made him desperate that he would never come to see her again but by the garden wall; that something, tonight – what was it? – was vastly becoming to her; that he devoutly hoped she would receive no one else; that his admiration for her was unbounded; that the stars, finally, had a curious pink light! He looked at her, through the flower-scented dusk, with admiring eyes; but he looked at the stars as well; he threw back his head and folded his arms, and let the conversation flag while he examined the firmament. He observed also the long shafts of light proceeding from the windows of the house, as they fell upon the lawn and played among the shrubbery. The Countess had always thought him a singular man, but tonight she thought him more singular than ever. She became satirical, and the point of her satire was that he was, after all, but a dull fellow; that his admiration was a poor compliment; that he would do well to turn his attention to astronomy! In answer to this he came perhaps (to the Countess's sense) as near as he had ever come to making a declaration.

'Dear lady,' he said, 'you don't begin to know how much I admire you!'

She left her place at this, and walked about her lawn, looking at him askance while he talked, trailing her embroidered robe over the grass, and fingering the folded petals of her flowers. He made a sort of sentimental profession of faith; he assured her that she represented his ideal of a certain sort of woman. This last phrase made her pause a moment and stare at him wide-eyed. 'Oh, I mean the finest sort,' he cried – 'the sort that exerts the widest sway! You represent the world and everything that the world can give, and you represent them at their best – in their most generous, most graceful most inspiring form. If a man were a revolutionist, you would reconcile him to society. You are a divine embodiment of all the amenities, the refinements, the complexities of life! You are the flower of urbanity, of culture, of tradition! You are the product of so many influences that it widens one's horizon to know you; of you too, it is true, that to admire you is a liberal education! Your charm is irresistible, I assure you I don't resist it!'

Compliments agreed with the Countess, as we may say; they not only made her happier, but they made her better. It became a matter of conscience with her to deserve them. These were magnificent ones, and she was by no means indifferent to them. Her cheek faintly flushed, her eyes vaguely glowed, and though her beauty, in the literal sense, was questionable, all that Benvolio said of her had never seemed more true. He said more in the same strain, and she listened without interrupting him. But at last she suddenly became impatient; it seemed to her that this was, after all, a tolerably inexpensive sort of wooing. But she did not betray her impatience with any petulance; she simply shook her finger a moment, to enjoin silence, and then she said, in a voice of extreme gentleness – 'You have too much imagination!' He answered that, to do her perfect justice, he had too little. To this she replied that it was not of her any longer he was talking; he had left her far behind. He was spinning fancies about some highly-subtilised figment of his brain. The best answer to this, it seemed to Benvolio, was to seize her hand and kiss it. I don't know what the Countess thought of this form of argument; I incline to think it both pleased and vexed her; it was at once too much and too little. She snatched her hand away and went rapidly into the house. Although Benvolio immediately followed her he was unable to overtake her; she had retired into impenetrable seclusion. A short time afterwards she left town, and went for the summer to an estate which she possessed in a distant part of the country.

Chapter 3

BENVOLIO WAS extremely fond of the country, but he remained in town after all his friends had departed. Many of them made him promise that he would come and see them. He promised, or half promised, but when he reflected that in almost every case he would find a house full of fellow-guests, to whose pursuits he would have to conform, and that if he rambled away with a valued duodecimo in his pocket to spend the morning alone in the woods, he would be denounced as a marplot and a selfish brute, he felt no great desire to pay visits. He had, as we know, his moods of expansion and of contraction; he had been tolerably inflated for many months past, and now he had begun to take in sail. And then I suspect the foolish fellow had no money to travel withal. He had lately put all his available funds into the purchase of a picture – an estimable work of the Venetian school, which had been suddenly thrown into the market. It was offered for a moderate sum, and Benvolio, who was one of the first to see it, secured it, and hung it triumphantly in his room. It had all the classic Venetian glow, and he used to lie on his divan by the hour, gazing at it. It had, indeed, a peculiar property, of which I have known no other example. Most pictures that are remarkable for their colour (especially if they have been painted for a couple of centuries) need a flood of sunshine on the canvas to bring it out. But this remarkable work seemed to have a hidden radiance of its own, which showed brightest when the room was half darkened. When Benvolio wished especially to enjoy his treasure he dropped his Venetian blinds, and the picture bloomed out into the cool dusk with enchanting effect. It represented, in a fantastic way, the story of Perseus and Andromeda – the beautiful naked maiden chained to a rock, on which, with picturesque incongruity, a wild fig-tree was growing; the green Adriatic tumbling at her feet, and a splendid brown-limbed youth in a curious helmet hovering near her on a winged horse. The journey his fancy made as he lay and looked at his picture Benvolio preferred to any journey he might make by the public conveyances.

But he resorted for entertainment, as he had often done before, to the windows overlooking the old garden behind his house. As the summer deepened, of course the charm of the garden increased. It grew more tangled and bosky and mossy, and sent forth sweeter and heavier odours into the neighbouring air. It was a perfect solitude; Benvolio had never seen a visitor there. One day, therefore, at this time, it puzzled him most agreeably to perceive a young girl sitting under one of the trees. She sat there a long time, and though she was at a distance, he managed, by looking long enough, to make out that she was pretty. She was dressed in black, and when she left her place her step had a kind of nun-like gentleness and demureness. Although she was alone, there was something timid and tentative in her movements. She wandered away and disappeared from sight, save that here and there he saw her white parasol gleaming in the gaps of the foliage. Then she came back to her seat under the great tree, and remained there for some time, arranging in her lap certain flowers that she had gathered. Then she rose again and vanished, and Benvolio waited in vain for her return. She had evidently gone into the house. The next day he saw her again, and the next, and the next. On these occasions she had a book in her hand, and she sat in her former place a long time, and read it with an air of great attention. Now and then she raised her head and glanced toward the house, as if to keep something in sight which divided her care; and once or twice she laid down her book and tripped away to her hidden duties with a lighter step than she had shown the first day. Benvolio formed a theory that she had an invalid parent or a relation of some kind, who was unable to walk, and had been moved into a window overlooking the garden. She always took up her book again when she came back, and bent her pretty head over it with charming earnestness. Benvolio had already discovered that her head was pretty. He fancied it resembled a certain exquisite little head on a Greek silver coin which lay, with several others, in an agate cup on his table. You see he had also already taken to fancying, and I offer this as the excuse for his staring at his modest neighbour by the hour. But he was not during these hours idle, because he was – I can't say falling in love with her; he knew her too little for that, and besides, he was in love with the Countess – but because he was at any rate cudgelling his brains about her. Who was she? what was she? why had he never seen her before! The house in which she apparently lived was in another street from Benvolio's own, but he went out of his way on purpose to look at it. It was an ancient, grizzled, sad-faced structure, with grated windows on the ground floor: it looked like a convent or a prison. Over a wall, beside it, there tumbled into the street some stray tendrils of a wild creeper from Benvolio's garden. Suddenly Benvolio began to suspect that the book the young girl in the garden was reading was none other than a volume of his own, put forth some six months before. His volume had a white cover and so had this; white covers are rather rare, and there was nothing impossible either in this young lady's reading his book or in her finding it interesting. Very many other women had done the same. Benvolio's neighbour had a pencil in her pocket which she every now and then drew forth, to make with it a little mark on her page. This quiet gesture gave the young man an exquisite pleasure.

I am ashamed to say how much time he spent, for a week, at his window. Every day the young girl came into the garden. At last there occurred a rainy day – a long warm summer's rain – and she stayed within doors. He missed her quite acutely, and wondered, half-smiling, half-frowning, that her absence should make such a difference for him.

He actually depended upon her. He was ignorant of her name; he knew neither the colour of her eyes nor the shade of her hair, nor the sound of her voice; it was very likely that if he were to meet her face to face, elsewhere, he would not recognise her. But she interested him; he liked her; he found her little indefinite black-dressed figure sympathetic. He used to find the Countess sympathetic, and certainly the Countess was as unlike this quiet garden-nymph as she could very well be and be yet a charming woman. Benvolio's sympathies, as we know, were large. After the rain the young girl came out again, and now she had another book, having apparently finished Benvolio's. He was gratified to observe that she bestowed upon this one a much more wandering attention. Sometimes she let it drop listlessly at her side, and seemed to lose herself in maidenly reverie. Was she thinking how much more beautiful Benvolio's verses were than others of the day? Was she perhaps repeating them to herself? It charmed Benvolio to suppose she might be; for he was not spoiled in this respect. The Countess knew none of his poetry by heart; she was nothing of a reader. She had his book on her table, but he once noticed that half the leaves were uncut.

After a couple of days of sunshine the rain came back again, to our hero's infinite annoyance, and this time it lasted several days. The garden lay dripping and desolate; its charm had quite departed. These days passed gloomily for Benvolio; he decided that rainy weather, in summer, in town, was intolerable. He began to think of the Countess again – he was sure that over her broad lands the summer sun was shining. He saw them, in envious fancy, studded with joyous Watteau-groups, feasting and making music under the shade of ancestral beeches. What a charming life! he thought – what brilliant, enchanted, memorable days! He had said the very reverse of all this, as you remember, three weeks before. I don't know that he had ever devoted a formula to the idea that men of imagination are not bound to be consistent, but he certainly conformed to its spirit. We are not, however, by any means at the end of his inconsistencies. He immediately wrote a letter to the Countess, asking her if he might pay her a visit.

Shortly after he had sent his letter the weather mended, and he went out for a walk. The sun was near setting the streets were all ruddy and golden with its light, and the scattered rain-clouds, broken into a thousand little particles, were flecking the sky like a shower of opals and amethysts. Benvolio stopped, as he sauntered along, to gossip a while with his friend the bookseller. The bookseller was a foreigner and a man of taste; his shop was in the arcade of the great square.

When Benvolio went in he was serving a lady, and the lady was dressed in black. Benvolio just now found it natural to notice a lady who was dressed in black, and the fact that this lady's face was averted made observation at once more easy and more fruitless. But at last her errand was finished; she had been ordering several books, and the bookseller was writing down their names. Then she turned round, and Benvolio saw her face. He stood staring at her most inconsiderately, for he felt an immediate certainty that she was the bookish damsel of the garden. She gave a glance round the shop, at the books on the walls, at the prints and busts, the apparatus of learning, in various forms, that it contained, and then, with the soundless, half-furtive step which Benvolio now knew so well, she took her departure. Benvolio seized the startled bookseller by the two hands and besieged him with questions. The bookseller, however, was able to answer but few of them. The young girl had been in his shop but once before, and had simply left an address, without any name. It was the address of which Benvolio had assured himself. The books she had ordered were all learned works – disquisitions on philosophy, on history, on the natural sciences, matters, all of them, in which she seemed an expert. For some of the volumes that she had just bespoken the bookseller was to send to foreign countries; the others were to be despatched that evening to the address which the young girl had left. As Benvolio stood there the old bibliophile gathered these latter together, and while he was so engaged he uttered a little cry of distress: one of the volumes of a set was missing. The work was a rare one, and it would be hard to repair the loss. Benvolio on the instant had an inspiration; he demanded leave of his friend to act as messenger: he himself would carry the books as if he came from the shop, and he would explain the absence of the lost volume, and the bookseller's views about replacing it, far better than one of the hirelings. He asked leave, I say, but he did not wait till it was given; he snatched up the pile of books and strode triumphantly away!

Chapter 4

As THERE WAS NO NAME on the parcel, Benvolio, on reaching the old gray house over the wall of whose court an adventurous tendril stretched its long arm into the street, found himself wondering in what terms he should ask to have speech of the person for whom the books were intended. At any hazard he was determined not to retreat until he had caught a glimpse of the interior and its inhabitants; for this was the same man, you must remember, who had scaled the moonlit wall of the Countess's garden. An old serving woman in a quaint cap answered his summons and stood blinking out at the fading daylight from a little wrinkled white face, as if she had never been compelled to take so direct a look at it before. He informed her that he had come from the bookseller's, and that he had been charged with a personal message for the venerable gentleman who had bespoken the parcel. Might he crave license to speak with him? This obsequious phrase was an improvisation of the moment – he had shaped it on the chance. But Benvolio had an indefinable conviction that it would fit the case; the only thing that surprised him was the quiet complaisance of the old woman.

'If it's on a bookish errand you come, sir,' she said, with a little wheezy sigh, 'I suppose I only do my duty in admitting you!'

She led him into the house, through various dusky chambers, and at last ushered him into an apartment of which the side opposite to the door was occupied by a broad low casement. Through its small old panes there came a green dim light – the light of the low western sun shining through the wet trees of the famous garden. Everything else was ancient and brown; the walls were covered with tiers upon tiers of books. Near the window, in the still twilight, sat two persons, one of whom rose as Benvolio came in. This was the young girl of the garden – the young girl who had been an hour since at the bookseller's. The other was an old man, who turned his head, but otherwise sat motionless.

Both his movement and his stillness immediately announced to Benvolio's quick perception that he was blind. In his quality of poet Benvolio was inventive; a brain that is constantly tapped for rhymes is tolerably alert. In a few moments' therefore, he had given a vigorous push to the wheel of fortune. Various things had happened. He had made a soft, respectful speech, he hardly knew about what; and the old man had told him he had a delectable voice – a voice that seemed to belong rather to a person of education than to a tradesman's porter. Benvolio confessed to having picked up an education, and the old man had thereupon bidden the young girl offer him a seat. Benvolio chose his seat where he could see her, as she sat at the low-browed casement. The bookseller in the square thought it likely Benvolio would come back that evening and give him an account of his errand, and before he closed his shop he looked up and down the street, to see whether the young man was approaching. Benvolio came, but the shop was closed. This he never noticed, however; he walked three times round all the arcades without noticing it. He was thinking of something else. He had sat all the evening with the blind old scholar and his daughter, and he was thinking intently, ardently, of them. When I say of them, of course I mean of the daughter.

A few days afterwards he got a note from the Countess saying it would give her pleasure to receive his visit. He immediately wrote to her that, with a thousand regrets, he found himself urgently occupied in town, and must beg leave to defer his departure for a day or two. The regrets were perfectly sincere, but the plea was none the less valid. Benvolio had become deeply interested in his tranquil neighbours, and, for the moment, a certain way the young girl had of looking at him – fixing her eyes, first with a little vague, half-absent smile, on an imaginary point above his head, and then slowly dropping them till they met his own – was quite sufficient to make him happy. He had called once more on her father, and once more, and yet once more, and he had a vivid provision that he should often call again. He had been in the garden, and found its mild mouldiness even more delightful on a nearer view. He had pulled off his very ill-fitting mask, and let his neighbours know that his trade was not to carry parcels, but to scribble verses. The old man had never heard of his verses; he read nothing that had been published later than the sixth century; and nowadays he could read only with his daughter's eyes. Benvolio had seen the little white volume on the table, and assured himself it was his own; and he noted the fact that in spite of its well-thumbed air the young girl had never given her father a hint of its contents. I said just now that several things had happened in the first half-hour of Benvolio's first visit. One of them was that this modest maiden fell in love with our young man. What happened when she learned that he was the author of the little white volume, I hardly know how to express; her innocent passion began to throb and flutter. Benvolio possessed an old quarto volume bound in Russia leather, about which there clung an agreeable pungent odour. In this old quarto he kept a sort of diary – if that can be called a diary in which a whole year had sometimes been allowed to pass without an entry. On the other hand, there were some interminable records of a single day. Turning it over you would have chanced, not unfrequently, upon the name of the Countess; and at this time you would have observed on every page some mention of 'the Professor' and of a certain person named Scholastica. Scholastica, you will immediately guess, was the Professor's daughter. Probably this was not her own name, but it was the name by which Benvolio preferred to know her, and we need not be more exact than he. By this time, of course, he knew a great deal about her, and about her venerable sire.

The Professor, before the loss of his eyesight and his health, had been one of the stateliest pillars of the University. He was now an old man; he had married late in life. When his infirmities came upon him he gave up his chair and his classes and buried himself in his library. He made his daughter his reader and his secretary, and his prodigious memory assisted her clear young voice and her softly-moving pen. He was held in great honour in the scholastic world; learned men came from afar to consult the blind sage and to appeal to his wisdom as to the ultimate law. The University settled a pension upon him, and he dwelt in a dusky corner, among the academic shades. The pension was small but the old scholar and the young girl lived with conventional simplicity. It so happened, however, that he had a brother, or rather a half-brother, who was not a bookish man, save as regarded his ledger and day-book. This personage had made money in trade, and had retired, wifeless and childless, into the old gray house attached to Benvolio's garden. He had the reputation of a skinflint, a curmudgeon, a bloodless old miser who spent his days in shuffling about his mouldy mansion making his pockets jingle, and his nights in lifting his money-bags out of trap-doors and counting over his hoard. He was nothing but a chilling shadow, an evil name, a pretext for a curse; no one had ever seen him, much less crossed his threshold. But it seemed that he had a soft spot in his heart. He wrote one day to his brother, whom he had not seen for years, that the rumour had come to him that he was blind, infirm, and poor; that he himself had a large house with a garden behind it; and that if the Professor were not too proud, he was welcome to come and lodge there. The Professor had come, in this way, a few weeks before, and though it would seem that to a sightless old ascetic all lodgings might be the same, he took a great satisfaction in his new abode. His daughter found it a paradise compared with their two narrow chambers under the old gable of the University, where, amid the constant coming and going of students, a young girl was compelled to lead a cloistered life.

Benvolio had assigned as his motive for intrusion, when he had been obliged to acknowledge his real character, an irresistible desire to ask the old man's opinion on certain knotty points of philosophy. This was a pardonable fiction, for the event, at any rate justified it. Benvolio, when he was fairly launched in a philosophical discussion, was capable of forgetting that there was anything in the world but metaphysics; he revelled in transcendent abstractions, and became unconscious of all concrete things – even of that most brilliant of concrete things, the Countess. He longed to embark on a voyage of discovery on the great sea of pure reason. He knew that from such voyages the deep-browed adventurer rarely returns; but if he were to find an El Dorado of thought, why should he regret the dusky world of fact? Benvolio had high colloquies with the Professor, who was a devout Neo-Platonist, and whose venerable wit had spun to subtler tenuity the ethereal speculations of the Alexandrian school. Benvolio at this season declared that study and science were the only game in life worth the candle, and wondered how he could ever for an instant have cared for more vulgar exercises. He turned off a little poem in the style of Milton's *Pensoroso*, which, if it had not quite the merit of that famous effusion, was at least the young man's own happiest performance. When Benvolio liked a thing he liked it as a whole – it appealed to all his senses. He relished its accidents, its accessories, its material envelope. In the satisfaction he took in his visits to the Professor it would have been hard to say where the charm of philosophy began or ended. If it began with a glimpse of the old man's mild, sightless blue eyes, sitting fixed beneath his shaggy white brows like patches of pale winter sky under a high-piled cloud, it hardly ended before it reached the little black bow on Scholastica's slipper; and certainly it had taken a comprehensive sweep in the interval. There was nothing in his friends that had not a charm, an interest, a character, for his appreciative mind. Their seclusion, their stillness, their super-simple notions of the world and the world's ways, the faint, musty perfume of the University which hovered about them, their brown old apartment, impenetrable to the rumours of the town – all these things were part of his entertainment. Then the essence of it perhaps was that if this silent simple life, the intellectual key, if you touched it, was so finely resonant. In the way of thought there was nothing into which his friends were not initiated – nothing they could not understand. The mellow light of their low-browed room, streaked with the moted rays that slanted past the dusky book-shelves, was the atmosphere of intelligence. All this made them, humble folk as they were, not so simple as they at first appeared. They, too, in their own fashion, knew the world; they were not people to be patronised; to visit them was not a condescension, but a privilege.

In the Professor this was not surprising. He had passed fifty years in arduous study, and it was proper to his character and his office that he should be erudite and venerable. But his devoted little daughter seemed to Benvolio at first almost grotesquely wise. She was an anomaly, a prodigy, a charming monstrosity. Charming, at any rate, she was, and as pretty, I must lose no more time in saying, as had seemed likely to Benvolio at his window. And yet, even on a nearer view, her prettiness shone forth slowly. It was as if it had been covered with a series of film-like veils, which had to be successively drawn aside. And then it was such a homely, shrinking, subtle prettiness, that Benvolio, in the private record I have mentioned, never thought of calling it by the arrogant name of beauty. He called it by no name at all; he contented himself with enjoying it – with looking into the young girl's mild gray eyes and saying things, on purpose, that caused her candid smile to deepen until (like the broadening ripple of a lake) it reached a particular dimple in her left cheek. This was its maximum; no smile could do more, and Benvolio desired nothing better. Yet I cannot say he was in love with the young girl; he only liked her. But he liked her, no doubt, as a man likes a thing but once in his life. As he knew her better, the oddity of her great learning quite faded away; it seemed delightfully natural, and he only wondered why there were not more women of the same pattern. Scholastica had imbibed the wine of science instead of her mother's milk. Her mother had died in her infancy, leaving her cradled in an old folio, three-quarters opened, like a wide V. Her father had been her nurse, her playmate, her teacher, her life-long companion, her only friend. He taught her the Greek alphabet before she knew her own, and fed her with crumbs from his scholastic revels. She had taken submissively what was given her, and, without knowing it, she grew up a little handmaid of science.

Benvolio perceived that she was not in the least a woman of genius. The passion for knowledge, of its own motion, would never have carried her far. But she had a perfect understanding – a mind as clear and still and natural as a woodland pool, giving back an exact and definite image of everything that was presented to it. And then she was so teachable, so diligent, so indefatigable. Slender and meagre as she was, and rather pale too, with being much within doors, she was never tired, she never had a headache, she never closed her book or laid down a pen with a sigh. Benvolio said to himself that she was exquisitely constituted for helping a man. What a work he might do on summer mornings and winter nights with that brightly demure little creature at his side, transcribing, recollecting, sympathising! He wondered how much she cared for these things herself; whether a woman could care for them without being dry and harsh. It was in a great measure for information on this point that he used to question her eyes with the frequency that I have mentioned. But they never gave him a perfectly direct answer, and this was why he came and came again. They seemed to him to say, 'If you could lead a student's life for my sake, I could be a life-long household scribe for yours.' Was it divine philosophy that made Scholastica charming, or was it she that made philosophy divine? I cannot relate everything that came to pass between these young people, and I must leave a great deal to your imagination. The summer waned and when the autumn afternoons began to grow vague the quiet couple in the old gray house had expanded to a talkative trio. For Benvolio the days had passed very fast; the trio had talked of so many things. He had spent many an hour in the garden with the young girl, strolling in the weedy paths, or resting on a moss-grown bench. She was a delightful listener, because she not only attended, but she followed. Benvolio had known women to fix very beautiful eyes upon him, and watch with an air of ecstasy the movement of his lips, and yet had found them, three minutes afterwards, quite incapable of saying what he was talking about. Scholastica gazed at him, but she understood him too.

Chapter 5

YOU WILL SAY THAT my description of Benvolio has done him injustice, and that, far from being the sentimental weathercock I have depicted, he is proving himself a model of constancy. But mark the sequel! It was at this moment precisely, that, one morning, having gone to bed the night before singing paeans to divine philosophy, he woke up with a headache, and in the worst of humours with abstract science. He remembered Scholastica telling him that she never had headaches, and the memory quite annoyed him. He suddenly found himself thinking of her as a neat little mechanical toy, wound up to turn pages and write a pretty hand, but with neither a head nor a heart that was capable of human ailments. He fell asleep again, and in one of those brief but vivid dreams that sometimes occur in the morning hours, he had a brilliant vision of the Countess. *She* was human beyond a doubt, and duly familiar with headaches and heartaches. He felt an irresistible desire to see her and to tell her that he adored her. This satisfaction was not unattainable, and before the day was over he was well on his way toward enjoying it. He left town and made his pilgrimage to her estate, where he found her holding her usual court, and leading a merry life. He had meant to stay with her a week; he stayed two months – the most entertaining months he had ever known I cannot pretend, of course, to enumerate the diversions of this fortunate circle, or to say just how Benvolio spent every hour of his time. But if the summer had passed quickly with him, the autumn moved with a tread as light. He

thought once in a while of Scholastica and her father – once in a while,
I say, when present occupations suffered his thoughts to wander. This
was not often, for the Countess had always, as the phrase is, a hundred
arrows in her quiver. You see, the negative, with Benvolio, always
implied as distinct a positive, and his excuse for being inconstant on
one side was that he was at such a time very assiduous on another. He
developed at this period a talent as yet untried and unsuspected, he
proved himself capable of writing brilliant dramatic poetry. The long
autumn evenings, in a great country house, were a natural occasion for
the much-abused pastime known as private theatricals. The Countess
had a theatre, and abundant material for a troupe of amateur players:
all that was lacking was a play exactly adapted to her resources. She
proposed to Benvolio to write one; the idea took his fancy; he shut
himself up in the library, and in a week produced a masterpiece. He
had found the subject one day when he was pulling over the Countess's
books, in an old MS. chronicle written by the chaplain of one of her
late husband's ancestors. It was the germ of an admirable drama, and
Benvolio greatly enjoyed his attempt to make a work of art of it. All his
genius, all his imagination, went into it. This was the proper mission of
his faculties, he cried to himself – the study of warm human passions,
the painting of rich dramatic pictures, not the dry chopping of logic.
His play was acted with brilliant success, the Countess herself repre-
senting the heroine. Benvolio had never seen her don the buskin, and
had no idea of her aptitude for the stage; but she was inimitable, she
was a natural artist. What gives charm to life, Benvolio hereupon said
to himself, is the element of the unexpected; and this one finds only in
women of the Countess's type. And I should do wrong to imply that he
here made an invidious comparison, for he did not even think of
Scholastica. His play was repeated several times, and people were
invited to see it from all the country round. There was a great bivouac
of servants in the castle court; in the cold November nights a bonfire
was lighted to keep the servants warm. It was a great triumph for
Benvolio, and he frankly enjoyed it. He knew he enjoyed it, and how
great a triumph it was, and he felt every disposition to drain the cup to
the last drop. He relished his own elation, and found himself excellent
company. He began immediately another drama – a comedy this
time – and he was greatly interested to observe that when his work was
on the stocks he found himself regarding all the people about him as
types and available figures. Everything he saw or heard was grist to his
mill; everything presented itself as possible material. Life on these
terms became really very interesting, and for several nights the laurels

of Molière kept Benvolio awake.

Delightful as this was, however, it could not last for ever. When the winter nights had begun the Countess returned to town, and Benvolio came back with her, his unfinished comedy in his pocket. During much of the journey he was silent and abstracted, and the Countess supposed he was thinking of how he should make the most of that capital situation in his third act. The Countess's perspicacity was just sufficient to carry her so far – to lead her, in other words, into plausible mistakes. Benvolio was really wondering what in the name of mystery had suddenly become of his inspiration, and why the witticisms in his play and his comedy had begun to seem as mechanical as the cracking of the post-boy's whip. He looked out at the scrubby fields, the rusty woods, the sullen sky, and asked himself whether *that* was the world to which it had been but yesterday his high ambition to hold up the mirror. The Countess's *dame de compagnie* sat opposite to him in the carriage. Yesterday he thought her, with her pale discreet face, and her eager movements that pretended to be indifferent a finished specimen of an entertaining genus. Today he could only say that if there was a whole genus it was a thousand pities, for the poor lady struck him as miserably false and servile. The real seemed hideous, he felt home-sick for his dear familiar rooms between the garden and the square, and he longed to get into them and bolt his door and bury himself in his old arm-chair and cultivate idealism for evermore. The first thing he actually did on getting into them was to go to the window and look out into the garden. It had greatly changed in his absence, and the old maimed statues, which all the summer had been comfortably muffled in verdure, were now, by an odd contradiction of propriety, standing white and naked in the cold. I don't exactly know how soon it was that Benvolio went back to see his neighbours. It was after no great interval, and yet it was not immediately. He had a bad conscience, and he was wondering what he should say to them. It seemed to him now (though he had not thought of it sooner) that they might accuse him of neglecting them. He had appealed to their friendship, he had professed the highest esteem for them, and then he had turned his back on them without farewell, and without a word of explanation. He had not written to them; in truth, during his sojourn with the Countess, it would not have been hard for him to persuade himself that they were people he had only dreamed about, or read about, at most, in some old volume of memoirs. People of their value, he could now imagine them saying, were not to be taken up and dropped for a fancy; and if friendship was not to be friendship as they themselves understood it, it was better that he should forget them at once and for ever. It is perhaps too much to affirm that he imagined them saying all this, they were too mild and civil, too unused to acting in self-defence. But they might easily receive him in a way that would imply a delicate resentment Benvolio felt profaned, dishonoured, almost contaminated; so that perhaps when he did at last return to his friends, it was because that was the simplest way to be purified. How did they receive him? I told you a good way back that Scholastica was in love with him, and you may arrange the scene in any manner that best accords with this circumstance. Her forgiveness, of course, when once that chord was touched, was proportionate to her displeasure. But Benvolio took refuge both from his own compunction and from the young girl's reproaches, in whatever form these were conveyed, in making a full confession of what he was pleased to call his frivolity. As he walked through the naked garden with Scholastica, kicking the wrinkled leaves, he told her the whole story of his sojourn with the Countess. The young girl listened with bright intentness, as she would have listened to some thrilling passage in a romance; but she neither sighed, nor looked wistful, nor seemed to envy the Countess, or to repine at her own ignorance of the great world. It was all too remote for comparison; it was not, for Scholastica, among the things that might have been. Benvolio talked to her very freely about the Countess. If she liked it, he found on his side that it eased his mind, and as he said nothing that the Countess would not have been flattered by, there was no harm done. Although, however, Benvolio uttered nothing but praise of this distinguished lady, he was very frank in saying that she and her way of life always left him at the end in a worse humour than when they found him. They were very well in their way, he said, but their way was not his way – it only seemed so at moments. For him, he was convinced, the only real felicity was in the pleasures of study! Scholastica answered that it gave her high satisfaction to hear this, for it was her father's belief that Benvolio had a great aptitude for philosophical research, and that it was a sacred duty to cultivate so rare a faculty.

'And what is your belief?' Benvolio asked, remembering that the young girl knew several of his poems by heart.

Her answer was very simple. 'I believe you are a poet.'

'And a poet oughtn't to run the risk of turning pedant?'

'No,' she answered; 'a poet ought to run all risks – even that one which for a poet is perhaps most cruel. But he ought to escape them all!'

Benvolio took great satisfaction in hearing that the Professor deemed that he had in him the making of a philosopher, and it gave an impetus to the zeal with which he returned to work.

Chapter 6

OF COURSE EVEN the most zealous student cannot work always, and often, after a very philosophic day, Benvolio spent with the Countess a very sentimental evening. It is my duty as a veracious historian not to conceal the fact that he discoursed to the Countess about Scholastica. He gave such a puzzling description of her that the Countess declared that she must be a delightfully quaint creature, and that it would be vastly amusing to know her. She hardly supposed Benvolio was in love with this little book-worm in petticoats, but to make sure – if that might be called making sure – she deliberately asked him. He said No; he hardly saw how he could be, since he was in love with the Countess herself! For a while this answer satisfied her, but as the winter went by she began to wonder whether there were not such a thing as a man being in love with two women at once. During many months that followed Benvolio led a kind of double life. Sometimes it charmed him and gave him an inspiring sense of personal power. He haunted the domicile of his gentle neighbours, and drank deep of the garnered wisdom of the ages; and he made appearances as frequent in the Countess's drawing-room, where he played his part with magnificent zest and ardour. It was a life of alternation and contrast, and it really demanded a vigorous and elastic temperament. Sometimes his own seemed to him quite inadequate to the occasion – he felt fevered, bewildered, exhausted. But when it came to the point of choosing one thing or the other, it was impossible to give up either his worldly habits or his studious aspirations. Benvolio raged inwardly at the cruel limitations of the human mind, and declared it was a great outrage that a man should not be personally able to do everything he could imagine doing. I hardly know how she contrived it but the Countess was at this time a more engaging woman than she had ever been. Her beauty acquired an ampler and richer cast, and she had a manner of looking at you as she slowly turned away with a vague reproachfulness that was at the same time an encouragement, which had lighted a hopeless flame in many a youthful breast. Benvolio one day felt in the mood for finishing his comedy, and the Countess and her friends acted it. Its success was no less brilliant than that of its predecessor, and the manager of the theatre immediately demanded the privilege of producing it. You will hardly believe me, however, when I tell you that on the night that his comedy was introduced to the public, its eccentric author sat discussing the absolute and the relative with the Professor and his daughter. Benvolio had all winter been observing that Scholastica never looked so pretty as when she sat of a winter's night, plying a quiet needle in the mellow circle of a certain antique brass lamp. On the night in question he happened to fall a-thinking of this picture, and he tramped out across the snow for the express purpose of looking at it. It was sweeter even than his memory promised, and it banished every thought of his theatrical honours from his head. Scholastica gave him some tea and her tea, for mysterious reasons, was delicious; better, strange to say, than that of the Countess, who, however, it must be added, recovered her ground in coffee. The Professor's parsimonious brother owned a ship which made voyages to China, and brought him goodly chests of the incomparable plant. He sold the cargo for great sums, but he kept a chest for himself. It was always the best one, and he had at this time carefully measured out a part of his annual dole, made it into a little parcel, and presented it to Scholastica. This is the secret history of Benvolio's fragrant cups. While he was drinking them on the night I speak of – I am ashamed to say how many he drank – his name, at the theatre, was being tossed across the footlights to a brilliant, clamorous multitude, who hailed him as the redeemer of the national stage. But I am not sure that he even told his friends that his play was being acted. Indeed, this was hardly possible, for I meant to say just now that he had forgotten it.

It is very certain, however, that he enjoyed the criticisms the next day in the newspapers. Radiant and, jubilant, he went to see the Countess with half a dozen of them in his pocket. He found her looking terribly dark. She had been at the theatre, prepared to revel in his triumph – to place on his head with her own hand, as it were, the laurel awarded by the public; and his absence had seemed to her a sort of personal slight. Yet his triumph had nevertheless given her an exceeding pleasure, for it had been the seal of her secret hopes of him. Decidedly he was to be a great man, and this was not the moment for letting him go! At the same time, there was something noble in his indifference, his want of eagerness, his finding it so easy to forget his honours. It was only an intellectual Croesus, the Countess said to herself, who could afford to keep so loose an account with fame. But she insisted on knowing where he had been, and he told her he had been discussing philosophy and tea with the Professor.

'And was not the daughter there?' the Countess demanded.

'Most sensibly!' he cried. And then he added in a moment – 'I don't know whether I ever told you, but she's almost as pretty as you.'

The Countess resented the compliment to Scholastica much more than she enjoyed the compliment to herself. She felt an extreme curiosity to see this inky-fingered syren, and as she seldom failed, sooner or later, to compass her desires, she succeeded at last in catching a glimpse of her innocent rival. To do so she was obliged to set a great deal of machinery in motion. She induced Benvolio to give a lunch, in his rooms, to some ladies who professed a desire to see his works of art, and of whom she constituted herself the chaperon. She took care that he threw open a certain vestibule that looked into the garden, and here, at the window, she spent much of her time. There was but a chance that Scholastica would come forth into the garden, but it was a chance worth staking something upon. The Countess gave to it time and temper, and she was finally rewarded. Scholastica came out. The poor girl strolled about for half an hour, in profound unconsciousness that the Countess's fine eyes were devouring her. The impression she made was singular. The Countess found her both pretty and ugly: she did not admire her herself, but she understood that Benvolio might. For herself, personally, she detested her, and when Scholastica went in and she turned away from the window, her first movement was to pass before a mirror, which showed her something that, impartially considered, seemed to her a thousand times more beautiful. The Countess made no comments, and took good care Benvolio did not suspect the trick she had played him. There was something more she promised herself to do, and she impatiently awaited her opportunity.

In the middle of the winter she announced to him that she was going to spend ten days in the country: she had received the most attractive accounts of the state of things on her domain. There had been great snow-falls, and the sleighing was magnificent; the lakes and streams were solidly frozen, there was an unclouded moon, and the resident gentry were skating, half the night, by torch-light. The Countess was passionately fond both of sleighing and skating, and she found this picture irresistible. And then she was charitable, and observed that it would be a kindness to the poor resident gentry, whose usual pleasures were of a frugal sort, to throw open her house and give a ball or two, with the village fiddlers. Perhaps even they might organise a bear-hunt, an entertainment at which, if properly conducted, a lady might be present as spectator. The Countess told Benvolio all this one day as he sat with her in her boudoir, in the fire-light, during the hour that precedes dinner. She had said more than once that he must decamp – that she must go and dress; but neither of them had moved. She did not invite him to go with her to the country; she only watched him as he sat gazing with a frown at the fire-light – the crackling blaze of the great logs which had been cut in the Countess's bear-haunted forests. At last she rose impatiently, and fairly turned him out. After he had gone she stood for a moment looking at the fire, with the tip of her foot on the fender. She had not to wait long; he came back within the minute – came back and begged her leave to go with her to the country – to skate with her in the crystal moonlight, and dance with her to the sound of the village violins. It hardly matters in what terms his request was granted; the notable point is that he made it. He was her only companion, and when they were established in the castle the hospitality extended to the resident gentry was less abundant than had been promised. Benvolio, however, did not complain of the absence of it, because, for the week or so, he was passionately in love with his hostess. They took long sleigh-rides, and drank deep of the poetry of winter. The blue shadows on the snow, the cold amber lights in the west, the leafless twigs against the snow-charged sky, all gave them extraordinary pleasure. The nights were even better, when the great silver stars, before the moon-rise glittered on the polished ice, and the young Countess and her lover, firmly joining hands, launched themselves into motion and into the darkness, and went skimming for miles with their winged steps. On their return, before the great chimney-place in the old library, they lingered a while and drank little cups of wine heated with spices. It was perhaps here, cup in hand – this point is uncertain – that Benvolio broke through the last bond of his reserve, and told the Countess that he loved her, in a manner to satisfy her. To be his in all solemnity, his only and his for ever – this he explicitly, passionately, imperiously demanded of her. After this she gave her ball to her country neighbours, and Benvolio danced, to a boisterous, swinging measure, with a dozen ruddy beauties dressed in the fashions of the year before last. The Countess danced with the lusty male counterparts of these damsels, but she found plenty of chances to watch Benvolio. Toward the end of the evening she saw him looking grave and bored, with very much such a frown in his forehead as when he had sat staring at the fire that last day in her boudoir. She said to herself for the hundredth time that he was the strangest of mortals.

On their return to the city she had frequent occasions to say it again. He looked at moments as if he had repented of his bargain – as if it did not at all suit him that his being the Countess's only lover should involve her being his only mistress. She deemed now that she had acquired the right to make him give an account of his time, and he did not conceal the fact that the first thing he had done on reaching town was to go to see his eccentric neighbours. She treated him hereupon to a passionate outburst of jealousy; called Scholastica a dozen harsh names – a little dingy blue-stocking, a little underhand, hypocritical Puritan; demanded he should promise never to speak to her again, and summoned him to make a choice once for all. Would he belong to her, or to that odious little schoolmistress? It must be one thing or the other; he must take her or leave her; it was impossible she should have a lover who was so little to be depended upon. The Countess did not say this made her unhappy, but she repeated a dozen times that it made her ridiculous. Benvolio turned very pale; she had never seen him so before; a great struggle was evidently taking place within him. A terrible scene was the consequence. He broke out into reproaches and imprecations; he accused the Countess of being his bad angel, of making him neglect his best faculties, mutilate his genius, squander his life; and yet he confessed that he was committed to her, that she fascinated him beyond resistance, and that, at any sacrifice, he must still be her slave. This confession gave the Countess uncommon satisfaction, and made up in a measure for the unflattering remarks that accompanied it. She on her side confessed – what she had always been too proud to acknowledge hitherto – that she cared vastly for him, and that she had waited for long months for him to say something of this kind. They parted on terms which it would be hard to define – full of mutual resentment and devotion, at once adoring and hating each other. All this was deep and stirring emotion, and Benvolio, as an artist, always in one way or another found his profit in emotion, even when it lacerated or suffocated him. There was, moreover, a sort of elation in having burnt his ships behind him, and vowed to seek his fortune, his intellectual fortune, in the tumult of life and action. He did no work; his power of work, for the time at least, was paralysed. Sometimes this frightened him; it seemed as if his genius were dead, his career cut short; at other moments his faith soared supreme; he heard, in broken murmurs, the voice of the muse, and said to himself that he was only resting, waiting, storing up knowledge. Before long he felt tolerably tranquil again; ideas began to come to him, and the world to seem entertaining. He demanded of the Countess that, without further delay, their union should be solemnised. But the Countess, at that interview I have just related, had, in spite of her high spirit, received a great fright. Benvolio, stalking up and down with clenched hands and angry eyes, had seemed to her a terrible man to marry; and though she was conscious of a strong will of her own, as well as of robust nerves, she had shuddered at the thought that such scenes might often occur.

She had hitherto seen little but the mild and genial, or at most the joyous and fantastic side of her friend's disposition; but it now appeared that there was another side to be taken into account, and that if Benvolio had talked of sacrifices, these were not all to be made by him. They say the world likes its master – that a horse of high spirit likes being well ridden. This may be true in the long run; but the Countess, who was essentially a woman of the world, was not yet prepared to pay our young man the tribute of her luxurious liberty. She admired him more, now that she was afraid of him, but at the same time she liked him a trifle less. She answered that marriage was a very serious matter; that they had lately had a taste of each other's tempers; that they had better wait a while longer; that she had made up her mind to travel for a year, and that she strongly recommended him to come with her, for travelling was notoriously an excellent test of friendship.

Chapter 7

SHE WENT TO ITALY, and Benvolio went with her; but before he went he paid a visit to his other mistress. He flattered himself that he had burned his ships behind him but the fire was still visibly smouldering. It is true, nevertheless, that he passed a very strange half-hour with Scholastica and her father. The young girl had greatly changed; she barely greeted him; she looked at him coldly. He had no idea her face could wear that look; it vexed him to find it there. He had not been to see her for many weeks, and he now came to tell her that he was going away for a year; it is true these were not conciliatory facts. But she had taught him to think that she possessed in perfection the art of trustful resignation, of unprotesting, cheerful patience – virtues that sat so gracefully on her bended brow that the thought of their being at any rate supremely becoming took the edge from his remorse at making them necessary. But now Scholastica looked older as well as sadder, and decidedly not so pretty. Her figure was meagre, her movements were angular, her charming eye was dull. After the first minute he avoided this charming eye; it made him uncomfortable. Her voice she scarcely allowed him to hear. The Professor, as usual, was serene and frigid, impartial and transcendental. There was a chill in the air, a shadow between them. Benvolio went so far as to wonder that he had ever found a great attraction in the young girl, and his present disillusionment gave him even more anger than pain. He took leave abruptly and coldly, and puzzled his brain for a long time afterward over the mystery of Scholastica's reserve.

The Countess had said that travelling was a test of friendship; in this case friendship (or whatever the passion was to be called) promised for some time to resist the test. Benvolio passed six months of the liveliest felicity. The world has nothing better to offer to a man of sensibility than a first visit to Italy during those years of life when perception is at its keenest, when knowledge has arrived, and yet youth has not departed. He made with the Countess a long slow progress through the lovely land, from the Alps to the Sicilian sea; and it seemed to him that his imagination, his intellect, his genius, expanded with every breath, and rejoiced in every glance. The Countess was in an almost equal ecstasy, and their sympathy was perfect in all points save the lady's somewhat indiscriminate predilection for assemblies and receptions. She had a thousand letters of introduction to deliver, which entailed a vast deal of social exertion. Often, on balmy nights when he would have preferred to meditate among the ruins of the Forum, or to listen to the moonlit ripple of the Adriatic Benvolio found himself dragged away to kiss the hand of a decayed princess, or to take a pinch from the snuff-box of an epicurean cardinal. But the cardinals, the princesses, the ruins, the warm southern tides which seemed the voice of history itself – these and a thousand other things resolved themselves into an immense pictorial spectacle – the very stuff that inspiration is made of. Everything Benvolio had written before coming to Italy now appeared to him worthless; this was the needful stamp, the consecration of talent. One day, however, his felicity was clouded; by a trifle you will say, possibly; but you must remember that in men of Benvolio's disposition primary impulses are almost always produced by small accidents. The Countess, speaking of the tone of voice of some one they had met, happened to say that it reminded her of the voice of that queer little woman at home – the daughter of the blind professor. Was this pure inadvertence, or was it malicious design? Benvolio never knew, though he immediately demanded of her, in surprise, when and where she had heard Scholastica's voice. His whole attention was aroused; the Countess perceived it, and for a moment she hesitated. Then she bravely replied that she had seen the young girl in the musty old book-room where she spent her dreary life. At these words, uttered in a profoundly mocking tone, Benvolio had an extraordinary sensation. He was walking with the Countess in the garden of a palace, and they had just approached the low balustrade of a terrace which commanded a magnificent view. On one side were violet Apennines, dotted here and there with a gleaming castle or convent; on the other stood the great palace through whose galleries the two had just been strolling, with its walls incrusted with medallions and its cornice charged with statues. But Benvolio's heart began to beat; the tears sprang to his eyes; the perfect landscape around him faded away and turned to blankness, and there rose before him, distinctly, vividly present, the old brown room that looked into the dull northern garden, tenanted by the quiet figures he had once told himself that he loved. He had a choking sensation and a sudden overwhelming desire to return to his own country.

The Countess would say nothing more than that the fancy had taken her one day to go and see Scholastica. 'I suppose I may go where I please!' she cried in the tone of the great lady who is accustomed to believe that her glance confers honour wherever it falls. 'I am sure I did her no harm. She's a good little creature, and it's not her fault if she's so ridiculously plain.' Benvolio looked at her intently, but he saw that he should learn nothing from her that she did not choose to tell. As he stood there he was amazed to find how natural, or at least how easy, it was to disbelieve her. She had been with the young girl; that accounted for anything; it accounted abundantly for Scholastica's painful constraint. What had the Countess said and done? what infernal trick had she played upon the poor girl's simplicity? He helplessly wondered, but he felt that she could be trusted to hit her mark. She had done him the honour to be jealous, and in order to alienate Scholastica she had invented some ingenious calumny against himself. He felt sick and angry, and for a week he treated his companion with grim indifference. The charm was broken, the cup of pleasure was drained. This remained no secret to the Countess who was furious at the mistake she had made. At last she abruptly told Benvolio that the test had failed; they must separate; he would gratify her by taking his leave. He asked no second permission, but bade her farewell in the midst of her little retinue, and went journeying out of Italy with no other company than his thick-swarming memories and projects.

The first thing he did on reaching home was to repair to the Professor's abode. The old man's chair, for the first time, was empty, and Scholastica was not in the room. He went out into the garden, where, after wandering hither and thither, he found the young girl seated in a dusky arbour. She was dressed, as usual, in black; but her head was drooping, her empty hands were folded, and her sweet face was more joyless even than when he had last seen it. If she had been changed then, she was doubly changed now. Benvolio looked round, and as the Professor was nowhere visible, he immediately guessed the cause of her mourning aspect. The good old man had gone to join his immortal brothers, the classic sages, and Scholastica was utterly alone. She seemed frightened at seeing him, but he took her hand, and she let him sit down beside her. 'Whatever you were once told that made you think ill of me is detestably false,' he said. 'I have the tenderest friendship for you, and now more than ever I should like to show it.' She slowly gathered courage to meet his eyes; she found them reassuring, and at last, though she never told him in what way her mind had been poisoned, she suffered him to believe that her old confidence had come back. She told him how her father had died, and how, in spite of the philosophic maxims he had bequeathed to her for her consolation, she felt very lonely and helpless. Her uncle had offered her a maintenance, meagre but sufficient; she had the old serving-woman to keep her company, and she meant to live in her present abode and occupy herself with collecting her father's papers and giving them to the world according to a plan for which he had left particular directions. She seemed irresistibly tender and touching, and yet full of dignity and self-support. Benvolio fell in love with her again on the spot, and only abstained from telling her so because he remembered just in time that he had an engagement to be married to the Countess, and that this understanding had not yet been formally rescinded. He paid Scholastica a long visit, and they went in together and rummaged over her father's books and papers. The old scholar's literary memoranda proved to be extremely valuable; it would be a useful and interesting task to give them to the world. When Scholastica heard Benvolio's high estimate of them her cheek began to glow and her spirit to revive. The present, then, was secure, she seemed to say to herself, and she would have occupation for many a month. He offered to give her every assistance in his power, and in consequence he came daily to see her. Scholastica lived so much out of the world that she was not obliged to trouble herself about vulgar gossip. Whatever jests were aimed at the young man for his visible devotion to a mysterious charmer, he was very sure that her ear was never wounded by base insinuations. The old serving-woman sat in a corner, nodding over her distaff, and the two friends held long confabulations over yellow manuscripts in which the commentary, it must be confessed, did not always adhere very closely to the text. Six months elapsed, and Benvolio found an ineffable charm in this mild mixture of sentiment and study. He had never in his life been so long of the same mind; it really seemed as if, as the phrase is, the fold were taken for ever – as if he had done with the world and were ready to live henceforth in the closet. He hardly thought of the Countess, and they had no correspondence. She was in Italy, in Greece, in the East, in the Holy Land, in places and situations that taxed the imagination.

One day, in the darkness of the vestibule, after he had left Scholastica, he was arrested by a little old man of sordid aspect, of whom he could make out hardly more than a pair of sharply-glowing eyes and an immense bald head, polished like a ball of ivory. He was a quite terrible little figure in his way, and Benvolio at first was frightened. 'Mr Poet,' said the old man, 'let me say a single word. I give my niece a maintenance. She may do what she likes. But she forfeits every penny of her allowance and her expectations if she is fool enough to marry a fellow who scribbles rhymes. I am told they are sometimes an hour finding two that will match! Good evening, Mr Poet!' Benvolio heard a sound like the faint jingle of loose coin in a breeches pocket, and the old man abruptly retreated into his domiciliary gloom. Benvolio had never seen him before, and he had no wish ever to see him again. He had not proposed to himself to marry Scholastica, and even if he had, I am pretty sure he would now have taken the modest view of the matter, and decided that his hand and heart were an insufficient compensation for the relinquishment of a miser's fortune. The young girl never spoke of her uncle; he lived quite alone, apparently, haunting his upper chambers like a restless ghost, and sending her, by the old serving woman, her slender monthly allowance, wrapped up in a piece of old newspaper. It was shortly after this that the Countess at last came back. Benvolio had been taking one of those long walks to which he had always been addicted, and passing through the public gardens on his way home, he had sat down on a bench to rest. In a few moments a carriage came rolling by; in it sat the Countess – beautiful, sombre, solitary. He rose with a ceremonious salute, and she went her way. But in five minutes she passed back again, and this time her carriage stopped. She gave him a single glance, and he got in. For a week afterward Scholastica vainly awaited him. What had happened? It had happened that, though she had proved herself both false and cruel, the Countess again asserted her charm, and our precious hero again succumbed to it. But he resumed his visits to Scholastica after an interval of neglect not long enough to be unpardonable; the only difference was that now they were not so frequent.

My story draws to a close, for I am afraid you have already lost patience with the history of this amiable weathercock. Another year ran its course, and the Professor's manuscripts were arranged in great piles and almost ready for the printer. Benvolio had had a constant hand in the work, and had found it exceedingly interesting; it involved inquiries and researches of the most stimulating and profitable kind. Scholastica was very happy. Her friend was often absent for many days, during which she knew he was leading the great world's life; but she had learned that if she patiently waited, the pendulum would swing back, and he would reappear and bury himself in their books and papers and talk. And their talk, you may be sure, was not all technical; they touched on everything that came into their heads, and Benvolio by no means felt obliged to be silent about those mundane matters as to which a vow of personal ignorance had been taken for his companion. He took her into his poetic confidence, and read her everything he had written since his return from Italy. The more he worked the more he desired to work; and so, at this time, occupied as he was with editing the Professor's manuscripts, he had never been so productive on his own account. He wrote another drama, on an Italian subject, which was performed with magnificent success; and this production he discussed with Scholastica scene by scene and speech by speech. He proposed to her to come and see it acted from a covered box, where her seclusion would be complete. She seemed for an instant to feel the force of the temptation; then she shook her head with a frank smile, and said it was better not. The play was dedicated to the Countess, who had suggested the subject to him in Italy, where it had been imparted to her, as a family anecdote, by one of her old princesses. This easy, fruitful, complex life might have lasted for ever, but for two most regrettable events. *Might* have lasted I say; you observe I do not affirm it positively. Scholastica lost her peace of mind; she was suffering a secret annoyance. She concealed it as far as she might from her friend, and with some success, for although he suspected something and questioned her, she persuaded him that it was his own fancy. In reality it was no fancy at all, but the very uncomfortable fact that her shabby old uncle, the miser, was a terrible thorn in her side. He had told Benvolio that she might do as she liked, but he had recently revoked this amiable concession. He informed her one day, by means of an illegible note, scrawled with a blunt pencil on the back of an old letter, that her beggarly friend the Poet came to see her altogether too often; that he was determined she never should marry a crack-brained rhymester, and that he requested that before the sacrifice became too painful she would be so good as to dismiss Mr Benvolio. This was accompanied by an intimation, more explicit than gracious, that he opened his money-bags only for those who deferred to his incomparable wisdom. Scholastica was poor, and simple, and lonely, but she was proud, for all that, with a shrinking and unexpressed pride of her own, and her uncle's charity, proffered on these terms, became intolerably bitter to her soul. She sent him word that she thanked him for his past liberality, but she would no longer be a charge upon him. She said to herself that she could work; she had a superior education; many women, she knew, supported themselves. She even found something inspiring in the idea of going out into the world, of which she knew so little, to seek her fortune. Her great desire, however, was to keep her situation a secret from Benvolio, and to prevent his knowing the sacrifice she was making for him. This it is especially that proves she was proud. It so happened that circumstances made secrecy possible. I don't know whether the Countess had always an idea of marrying Benvolio, but her imperious vanity still suffered from the spectacle of his divided allegiance, and it suggested to her a truly malignant revenge. A brilliant political mission, to treat of a special question, was about to be despatched to a neighbouring government, and half a dozen young men of eminence were to be attached to it. The Countess had influence at Court, and without saying anything to Benvolio, she immediately urged his claim to a post, on the ground of his distinguished services to literature. She pulled her wires so cleverly that in a very short time she had the pleasure of presenting him his appointment on a great sheet of parchment, from which the royal seal dangled by a blue ribbon. It involved an exile of but a few weeks, and to this, with her eye on the sequel of her project, she was able to resign herself. Benvolio's imagination took fire at the thought of spending a month at a foreign court, in the very hotbed of consummate diplomacy; this was a phase of experience with which he was as yet unacquainted. He departed, and no sooner had he gone than the Countess, at a venture, waited upon Scholastica. She knew the girl was poor, and she believed that in spite of her homely virtues she would not, if the opportunity were placed before her in a certain light, prove implacably indisposed to better her fortunes. She knew nothing of the young girl's contingent expectations from her uncle, and her interference at this juncture was simply a remarkable coincidence. She laid before her a proposal from a certain great lady, whose husband, an eminent general, had just been dubbed governor of an island on the other side of the globe. This lady desired a preceptress for her children; she had heard of Scholastica's merit, and she ventured to hope that she might persuade her to accompany her to the Antipodes and reside in her family. The offer was brilliant; to Scholastica it seemed mysteriously and providentially opportune. Nevertheless she hesitated, and demanded time for reflection; without telling herself why, she wished to wait till Benvolio should return. He wrote her two or three letters, full of the echoes of his brilliant actual life, and without a word about the things that were nearer her own experience. The month elapsed, but he was still absent. Scholastica, who was in correspondence with the governor's wife, delayed her decision from week to week. She had sold her father's manuscripts to a publisher for a very small sum, and gone, meanwhile, to live in a convent. At last the governor's lady demanded her ultimatum. The poor girl scanned the horizon and saw no rescuing friend; Benvolio was still at the court of Illyria! What she saw was the Countess's fine eyes eagerly watching her over the top of her fan. They seemed to contain a horrible menace, and to hold somehow her happiness at their mercy. Her heart sank; she gathered up her few possessions and set sail, with her illustrious protectors, for the Antipodes. Shortly after her departure Benvolio returned. He felt a terrible pang of rage and grief when he learned that she had gone; he went to the Countess, prepared to accuse her of the basest treachery. But she checked his reproaches by arts that she had never gone so far as to use before, and promised him that, if he would trust her, he should never miss that pale-eyed little governess. It can hardly be supposed that he believed her; but he appears to have been guilty of letting himself be persuaded without belief. For some time after this he almost lived with the Countess. He had, with infinite pains, purchased from his neighbour, the miser, the right of occupancy of the late Professor's apartment. This repulsive proprietor, in spite of his constitutional aversion to rhymesters, had not resisted the financial argument, and seemed greatly amazed that a poet should have a dollar to spend. Scholastica had left all things in their old places, but Benvolio, for the present, never went into the room. He turned the key in the door, and kept it in his waistcoat-pocket, where, while he was with the Countess, his fingers fumbled with it. Several months rolled by, and the Countess's promise was not verified. He missed Scholastica woefully, and missed her more as time elapsed. He began at last to go to the old brown room and to try to do some work there. He only half succeeded in a fashion; it seemed dark and empty; doubly empty when he remembered what it might have been. Suddenly he ceased to visit the Countess; a long time passed without her seeing him. She met him at another house, and had some remarkable words with him. She covered him with reproaches that were doubtless deserved, but he made her an answer that caused her to open her eyes and flush, and admit afterward that, for a clever woman, she had been a great fool. 'Don't you see,' he said, 'can't you imagine, that I cared for you only by contrast? You took the trouble to kill the contrast, and with it you killed everything else. For a constancy I prefer *this*!' And he tapped his poetic brow. He never saw the Countess again.

I rather regret now that I said at the beginning of my story that it was not to be a fairy tale; otherwise I should be at liberty to relate, with harmonious geniality, that if Benvolio missed Scholastica he missed the Countess also, and led an extremely fretful and unproductive life, until one day he sailed for the Antipodes and brought Scholastica home. After this he began to produce again, only, many people said that his poetry had become dismally dull. But excuse me; I am writing as if it *were* a fairy tale!

WORDSWORTH CLASSICS

General Editors: Marcus Clapham and Clive Reynard
Titles in this series

DISTRIBUTION

AUSTRALIA, BRUNEI
& MALAYSIA
Reed Editions
22 Salmon Street, Port Melbourne
Vic 3207, Australia
Tel: (03) 646 6716
Fax (03) 646 6925

DENMARK
BOG-FAN
St. Kongensgade 61A
1264 København K

BOGPA SIKA
Industrivej 1, 7120 Vejle Ø

FRANCE
Bookking International
16 Rue des Grands Augustins
75006 Paris

GERMANY, AUSTRIA
& SWITZERLAND
Swan Buch-Marketing GmbH
Goldscheuerstrabe 16
D-7640 Kehl Am Rhein, Germany

GREAT BRITAIN & IRELAND
Wordsworth Editions Ltd
Cumberland House, Crib Street,
Ware, Hertfordshire SG12 9ET

Selecta Books
The Selectabook
Distribution Centre
Folly Road, Roundway, Devizes
Wiltshire SN10 2HR

HOLLAND & BELGIUM
Uitgeverlj en Boekhandel
Van Gennep BV, Spuistraat 283
1012 VR Amsterdam, Holland

INDIA
OM Book Service
1690 First Floor
Nai Sarak, Delhi – 110006
Tel: 3279823-3265303 Fax: 3278091

ITALY
Magis Books
Piazza Della Vittoria I/C
42100 Reggio Emilia
Tel: 0522-452303 Fax: 0522-452845

NEW ZEALAND
Whitcoulls Limited
Private Bag 92098, Auckland

NORWAY
Norsk Bokimport AS
Bertrand Narvesensvei 2
Postboks 6219, Etterstad, 0602 Oslo

PORTUGAL
Cashkeen Limited
(Isabel Leao) 25 Elmhurst Avenue
London N2 0LT
Tel: 081-444 3781 Fax: 081-444 3171

SINGAPORE
Book Station
18 Leo Drive, Singapore
Tel: 4511998 Fax: 4529188

SOUTH EAST CYPRUS
Tinkerbell Books
19 Dimitri Hamatsou Street, Paralimni
Famagusta, Cyprus
Tel: 03-8200 75

SOUTH WEST CYPRUS & GREECE
Huckleberry Trading
4 Isabella, Anavargos, Pafos, Cyprus
Tel: 06-231313

SOUTH AFRICA, ZIMBABWE
CENTRAL & E. AFRICA
Trade Winds Press (Pty) Ltd
P O Box 20194, Durban North 4016

SPAIN
Ribera Libros
Dr. Areilza No.19, 48011 Bilbao
Tel: 441-87-87 Fax: 441-80-29

USA, CANADA & MEXICO
Universal Sales & Marketing
230 Fifth Avenue, Suite 1212
New York, N Y 10001 USA
Tel: 212-481-3500 Fax: 212-481-3534

DIRECT MAIL
Redvers
Redvers House, 13 Fairmile,
Henley-on-Thames, Oxfordshire RG9 2JR
Tel: 0491 572656 Fax: 0491 573590